ii

Black Harvest
by
Alex Lukeman

Copyright 2012 by Alex Lukeman

iv

The PROJECT Series:

Acknowledgements

As always, the patience of my wife, Gayle. She sees many things I don't. Gloria, Penny, Tony-Paul, all of whom took the time to read and comment on earlier versions. Sandy Bresnahan for her comments.

Special thanks to Andrew Marino, who went beyond the call of duty. He used his writer's eye to look at the MS and make excellent suggestions that helped me create a better book. Thanks to readers. You make it worth the effort.

Blog: http://www.alexlukeman.blogspot.com
Website: http://www.alexlukeman.org

CHAPTER ONE

Sometimes it's better not to find what you're looking for.

The last gasp of a bitter New England winter clenched the campus at Dartmouth College in arctic cold, but inside Rauner Library it was warm and comfortable. James Campbell peered through a magnifying glass at what he'd found.

Nine reddish-brown clay tablets from ancient Persia, covered with writing. The marks were as clear and sharp as the day they had been pressed into the clay, almost 2400 years before. Campbell made a final note on his laptop computer and closed it down.

Campbell was a stout man in his 60s. He had gray hair thinning back in a widow's peak from a face creased with years of peering though microscopes at tiny life forms that heralded death and destruction. He'd seen nothing alive under his glass tonight. Only the tablets that he'd found buried in the archives. They held a clue to the fulfillment of a dream. Or a possible nightmare.

It could be the key, he thought.

Campbell made pictures of the tablets with his smart phone and composed two messages. A touch on the screen sent the emails and pictures on their way. He placed the phone and a copy of the writing in the case with his laptop. The tablets went back to their drawers in the restricted archives. He shrugged on his heavy coat, picked up the laptop and headed for the exit. It was late, but Campbell's status gave him access at any hour. A tired watchman rose from his chair and unlocked the door. There was a whiff of bourbon about him. Campbell stepped into the frigid night.

The ground crackled under his feet. The sky was a sea of brittle stars. Each breath of frozen air felt like the kiss of a razor, sharp and hurtful. He walked to his car, parked in the deserted lot. The windows were fogged. Odd, he thought, in this dry air.

The rented Volvo protested and started. Campbell waited for the engine to warm. He thought about the tablets.

Something sharp pressed across his throat. Adrenaline flooded his body.

"Don't move." In the rear view mirror, Campbell saw a dark face. The bones were narrow, the eyes hooded and dark.

"What..."

"Don't speak unless I tell you. Understand?"

"Yes."

"You've been researching something. Answer, yes or no?"

Campbell swallowed. The blade made a thin pain against his Adam's apple.

"Research. Yes."

"What have you found? I'll know if you lie. If you lie I'll cut off your ear. You believe me?"

"Yes." Something primal coursed down his spine, left over from an age when humans lived in caves. Fear.

"What have you found?"

"Records from Alexander's conquest of the Persian Empire, after he entered Babylon. Accounting from the King's treasuries."

"Nothing else?"

"No." Sweat started on his forehead.

Campbell screamed as his ear flew onto the floor. Blood poured down his neck. Before he could move the knife was back at his throat, wet with his own blood.

"You're not a historian. You lied. Don't do it again. Tell me what I want and you walk away."

The man hadn't hidden his face. Campbell knew he was going to die. He thought of his wife, ill at home. Sudden sadness brought tears to his eyes. What would she do?

Impotent thoughts of survival flooded his mind. Maybe he could twist away. Use the laptop or car keys as a weapon. Pull the knife from his throat before it cut him. Scream, open the door, roll away.

All useless.

Pain seared the side of his head. Blood ran down under his collar. He felt dizzy. The voice from behind was quiet. "I'm going to ask one more time. What have you found?"

Stall him. Maybe I can get my arm up in time.

"I swear, just lists of stores, what was in the treasury before the conquest. Records demanded by Alexander." That part was true. "Nothing of importance. It has all been seen before."

"Do you have the tablets with you?"

"No, they're in the library."

"In the library."

"Yes."

White fire slashed across his throat, through flesh and arteries and bone. Blood spurted over the windshield. Campbell grasped his throat with both hands, trying to stem the flood, choking on his life. He thrashed and gurgled and fell forward and died.

The man got out of the car, ignoring the mess slumped over the steering wheel. He went around the back, opened the front passenger door, took the laptop from the seat and walked away into the frozen night.

CHAPTER TWO

Nick Carter was done sleeping for the night. He'd had the dream about the grenade again. Now it was five in the morning. He waited for the sun to come up. Already on the third cup of coffee. He sat at the kitchen counter in his apartment and wondered why the dream kept coming back. It wasn't like he didn't understand why he had it.

Nick was Director of Special Operations for the Project, a black ops intelligence unit that reported only to the President. The title was a fancy way of saying he got to plan missions and call the shots in the field. He didn't get to say anything about how or when people might shoot at him. The real Director of the Project was Elizabeth Harker.

Right before Harker recruited him into the Project, back when he was recovering from the grenade that almost killed him, the shrink told him the dream was a way for his mind to try and work out an irresolvable inner conflict. That helped about as much as telling him the reason he had the dream was because he had the dream. The shrink had another term for it: cognitive dissonance. What happened when reality rammed head-on into belief and won. Shrinks always had a term for something.

He knew goddamned well why he had the dream. Since he knew it, why did he keep having it? He'd been down this road before, playing out the loop in his head. It never got anywhere.

To hell with it.

He got up, took eggs from the refrigerator, bread from the pantry. He got a pan from the drawer, turned on the stove and dropped butter in it. He popped the bread in the toaster, scrambled the eggs and dumped them in the pan.

As he ate he thought about the dream again.

They come in fast over the ridge, the rotors chop-chop-chop overhead, toward a miserable village baking in bright Afghan sun. A rough dirt street runs down the middle between the houses.

He's first out and hits the street running, M4 up by his cheek, his Marines stringing out hard behind him. Houses line both sides of the street, the walls pocked with holes from some long forgotten firefight. On his left is the market, a makeshift collection of ramshackle bins and hanging cloth walls. The butcher's stall is engulfed in flies.

He's in the market. He can smell the adrenaline sweat of his fear. He keeps away from the walls. A baby cries. The street is empty. Where are they?.

The rooftops fill with bearded men armed with AKs. The market stalls explode in a blizzard of splinters and plaster and rock fragmenting from the sides of the buildings.

A child runs toward him, screaming something about Allah. He has a grenade. Carter hesitates, it's a child. The boy is maybe ten years old. Maybe twelve. He cocks his arm back and throws as Nick shoots him. The boy's head explodes in a cloud of blood and bone. The grenade drifts toward him in slow motion...everything goes white...

Nick came back to the kitchen. He was sweating. He looked down at his hand, white knuckled around the coffee cup. His eggs were cold. The coffee was cold. He'd been gone, back in that village. That hadn't happened for awhile, not since Pakistan, right before Selena got shot.

That had been bad luck, running into a Taliban unit in a snowstorm after a bloody encounter in the high country of the Hindu Kush. Her armor had saved her. Barely. He'd carried her back to the LZ, hoping she'd be alive when he got there. She'd survived. That was what mattered.

Selena. He couldn't sort out his feelings about her and he was tired of thinking about it. He decided to go to work early and hit the gym. Before the traffic got bad.

The gym in the basement of Project headquarters smelled of sweat and stress and dry air from the heating system. Gyms weren't much fun anymore but his old wounds waited in the wings. If he didn't work out he'd lose his edge. The gym required no introspection. It was something he understood.

After an hour on the machines he began jumping rope. He caught himself in the big mirrors. Hard looking, six feet of tension, 200 pounds. Looking in the mirror he thought that if he didn't know who he was he might have scared himself. He wasn't going to win any awards for beauty, that was for sure.

He looked away from the mirror. His sweats were dark, he'd built up a good burn. His back was sore, but nothing he couldn't handle. No need to think about anything except the simple rhythm of his body, the smooth blurring of the rope.

It was good not to think.

Selena Connor came in. She watched Nick for a moment. A big, tough man. Not pretty, not ugly. Eyes that were gray with an odd fleck of gold. His face was tight with concentration. The scar on his left ear was red. It always got that way when he exercised. It got that way in the bedroom, too. She set her gym bag down on a bench and began stretching. He watched her as the rope circled in a figure eight around him.

"Hey," she said.

"Hey yourself. Almost done." He stepped up his pace. Selena looked good, even in dark blue sweats. Nick envied the athletic grace she brought to every movement. She finished her warm up and came over. A wisp of red blond hair fell across her forehead. Her violet eyes held a hint of mischief. Nick slowed and stopped.

She looked up at him. "Want to learn a few tricks? Brush up a little?"

Nick caught the challenge in her tone. He was good at unarmed combat, but Selena was way out of his class.

"If you think you can handle it."

"Me? Or you?"

Nick had sixty pounds and two inches on her. The sixth or seventh time Selena brought him to the mat, the thought crossed his mind he was getting a little old for this kind of brushing up. He ached all over from the beating he was getting.

"Okay, I give up. That's enough."

"You don't want to practice the wrist locks again?"

"I practice anymore, I won't have a wrist left to practice with."

She smiled. The corners of her mouth crinkled at the corners. It was a good smile. She picked up a towel, dabbed at her face. She'd hardly worked up a sweat.

"You're getting better. You almost had me once." The phone in her bag signaled a message. She went over to the bench, took out the phone and listened. After a minute she hung up and put the phone back in the bag.

"That was a friend of mine over at Georgetown, Kevin McCullough. He wants me to translate some pictures of cuneiform tablets."

Selena had a world reputation in ancient languages. Not many people could recite Beowulf in Anglo-Saxon. Not many would want to. Selena wasn't like most people.

"It figures you read Cuneiform. Any good books back then?"

"No books but good stories. Right up your alley. You might like them, they're full of blood and murder." She picked up the bag. "I'm going over there as soon as I shower. Want to come along?"

"To the shower?"

"Smart ass. No, to Georgetown."

"Sure. Harker will call if she wants us."

They took Selena's Mercedes down the Memorial Parkway, crossed the Key Bridge into Washington and drove to Georgetown University. They parked near Healy Hall, where Selena's friend has his office.

The hall would have looked right at home in London during the days of empire. It was massive, five stories high, built from blocks of gray stone. It had turrets and two large towers. Long rows of windows fronted the structure.

"Some building." Carter looked up at the central tower. He assumed it had bells. "Quasimodo would like it here."

"It does have a heavy feeling, doesn't it?"

"The turrets are a nice touch. Gives it that contemporary look."

McCullough's office was on the fourth floor. Nick could see something was wrong as soon as they went in. Professor McCullough was in his late fifties or early sixties. He was short, about five nine, with sparse red hair and a soft, pale face. He wore a soft brown jacket of fine wool. Watery blue eyes peered at them through bifocals.

"Selena, thank you for coming."

"Hello, Kevin. This is Nick Carter. We work together."

McCullough's palm was moist when Nick shook hands. The room was stuffy and hot. A large window looked out from the front of the building. It was closed. Papers were everywhere, in files, in boxes. A floor to ceiling bookshelf took up one wall, struggling with the weight of too many books. The room smelled of dust and dry paper. Looking at the chaos was enough to make Nick's eyes hurt. McCullough gestured at two battered chairs.

"Sit, please."

He took the chair behind his desk and gathered himself.

"Selena. The police called me." He twisted his fingers together.

"What's the matter, Kevin?"

"The pictures I want you to look at were sent by a friend, Jim Campbell. He was murdered last night. After he sent the pictures. Well, of course it was after. The police are calling his colleagues."

Selena and Nick glanced at each other.

"Kevin, I'm sorry."

"Jim was a good friend. We were in the same field."

"What is your field, Professor?" Nick scratched his ear.

"Microbiology. I specialize in crop viruses. Jim was one of the world's leading authorities. He was researching a collection of artifacts at Dartmouth College." He shook his head. "I can't get it through my head that someone killed him. Why would anyone want to do that?"

"What was he researching?" Selena asked.

"Cuneiform tablets found in Iraq. He was looking for clues to ancient famines, crop failures. Some of those killed hundreds of thousands of people. Jim worked for CDC in Atlanta. He was quite brilliant. He spent several years studying ancient languages just so he could work directly from the old sources."

Selena nodded. "I can understand that. Was there a message with the pictures?"

"Well, yes, there was. It's very odd. Jim said he was on the trail of something. He said I should have the writing translated and I should be careful."

"Why would he say that?"

"I haven't any idea. That's why I called you, to find out what's on the tablets. Right after that I heard from the police." McCullough was agitated.

"May I see the pictures?"

"I printed them for you." McCullough fumbled through papers on his desk and handed them to her. They were in black and white on cheap copy paper. Nick glanced over. The writing reminded him of ordered rows of chicken tracks.

She looked at the first page. "This style is from the fourth century BCE."

"That would correspond to Alexander's conquest of the Persian Empire."

"I'd need time for an accurate translation, but this looks like a fragment from one of the epic poems." She turned a page. "This part is different. It's from the treasury of Darius III in Babylon."

She traced the marks with her finger. "It's an accounting or inventory. Darius had an enormous treasure. Alexander used it to pay his troops."

"What would it be worth today?" Nick was curious.

"A lot." She turned a page. "Let's see...100,000 talents of gold and silver."

"What's a talent?"

"It's how they measured coins. By volume. A talent is around 25 liters."

She turned another page. "Whoever wrote this was very detailed. This is interesting. A golden container or urn, two cubits high, sealed, graven with a black horse and an inscription saying the urn contains the Curse of Demeter Erinys."

Nick opened his mouth to ask, but Selena beat him to it.

"A cubit is about eighteen inches."

"That's not what I was going to ask. Who's Demeter?"

"Demeter is the Greek goddess of the harvest."

She came to the last page. "I need to study this, but it looks like Alexander sent the urn and treasure off to Greece with someone. I wonder if any of it still exists?"

"Two and a half million liters of gold and silver and a big gold pot?" Nick looked at her. "If it did and Campbell knew something about it, people would kill for that."

McCullough seemed uncomfortable. A light knocking interrupted them. A student opened the door.

"Excuse me, Professor. This just came for you." He held an express delivery package in his hand.

"Thank you, William." McCullough took the package and placed it with the clutter on his desk.

"Selena, could you take this copy and translate it for me? Write it down?"

"I'd be happy to." She put the papers in her jacket pocket. McCullough saw the Glock in its quick draw holster under her tailored jacket.

"You carry a gun?" He seemed shocked.

"I'm a kind of federal agent now, Kevin. I translate things for the government. They insist I wear it. I'm not sure I'd know what to do with it."

Nick kept a straight face.

"Well." McCullough stood. "I have to get ready for my afternoon lecture. It's good to see you."

"I'll get the translation done in a day or two. We'll have coffee." She paused. "Kevin, it's probably a good idea not to mention this. Nick's right. It might have something to do with why your friend was murdered."

"Yes. All right. Goodbye, Mr. Carter."

Nick glanced back as they left. McCullough seemed dazed, pushing papers around on his desk, looking for his lecture notes.

They came out of Healy Hall and stopped by a large fountain. The sky was clear and blue, good weather after days of gray skies and drizzle.

"McCullough didn't like it when I told him someone might kill for that treasure."

"He's an academic, Nick."

"How does he get anything done in that mess up there?"

Selena was about to say something when the sky detonated in a thunderclap over their heads. The blast knocked them to the ground. The sound rolled away toward the Potomac. Debris rained on the lawns and parking lots and parked cars, rock and smoldering wood and bits of masonry. A flurry of paper drifted down from above.

"Jesus." Nick stood, helped Selena to her feet. Her knee was scraped and bleeding. Screams and shouts came from the building. They looked up.

A large part of the outer wall on the fourth floor was gone. Black smoke poured through the hole. Yellow and orange tongues of flame flickered in the darkness.

"That's where Kevin's office is. Right there."

"Not any more." He sniffed the air. "Smell that? That's an odor tag for Semtex. The package he just got was a bomb."

"Why?"

"Maybe the message he told us about. Someone killed his friend and now they've killed him. What else could it be?"

She felt her jacket pocket and the paper copy of the tablets. "We could have been there when it went off."

"Yeah, but we weren't."

She looked stricken. "Nick, Kevin had a wife and three grown kids. He was a sweet man. I can't believe this. What's so damned important about those tablets someone would want to kill him?"

"I guess we'll find out when you translate them. I'm sorry about your friend."

Selena looked up at the smoke pouring out of the fourth floor. People were streaming out of the building. Sirens sounded in the distance.

"What now?" she said.

"We go back to the Project before the cops get here."

"Shouldn't we tell them about that package?"

"They don't need us to figure it out. We need to talk with Harker."

They got into Selena's Mercedes. A man in a dented white pickup parked two rows away watched them leave. He noted the time and reached for his cell phone.

CHAPTER THREE

Project Director Elizabeth Harker was a small woman. She always dressed in black and white. Today she wore an all black linen suit with a white scarf tie at her throat. The suit matched her raven black hair. Her hair was artfully cut to frame the fine bones of her face. Her emerald green eyes were wide, cat-like. She had milk-white skin, small ears and a slim figure, like an elf or fairy sprite from a Shakespearean tale. Her looks tended to make self-important people dismiss her. It was a mistake they didn't make twice. Harker was no fairy sprite.

Harker's desk was wide and clean. She had a green desk blotter with leather corners. She had an antique ink stand and a silver pen that had belonged to FDR. There was a picture of the twin towers on 9/11 in a silver frame. A reminder.

Stephanie Willits sat between Nick and Selena. She had a wide, attractive face and dark eyes. This morning she'd chosen a red dress and white blouse and dangly gold earrings. There were three gold bracelets on her left wrist. Steph was responsible for all computer resources at the Project. She talked to her computers as if they were her family and could make the big Crays on the floor below do things no one else thought possible.

Nick couldn't put his finger on it, but she seemed different. She'd done something to her hair, but that wasn't it. She'd lightened up since Elizabeth had returned, but that wasn't it either. She seemed more alive. Even happy.

Harker played with her pen. "Selena, do you think McCullough was murdered because of the message from his friend?"

"It seems like too much of a coincidence."

"I wonder if the bomb was meant for you and Nick?"

Nick rubbed the scar on his left ear. A Chinese bullet had taken off the earlobe the first day he'd met Selena. Sometimes it burned like fire when everything was about to go bad. This time it was only an itch.

"It wasn't for us. No one knew we were going there. Besides, there are easier ways to take us out than blowing up a university. That bomb was Semtex, someone with serious resources like a terrorist group."

"You're sure it was Semtex."

"I'm sure."

"Steph, see if you can find out what the police in New Hampshire know about the murder up there."

"I'll do it now." She got up and left.

"I wouldn't bet on the local cops finding much," Nick said. "Whoever sent that bomb knew what they were doing. If they killed Campbell they won't have left clues."

"Why would someone target these men? Selena, I'd like a full translation on those notes McCullough gave you."

"I'll have it done later today."

Harker toyed with her pen and set it down. Picked it up again. Began tapping. Thinking. Carter watched her.

"The Bureau will be on it because of the bombing," she said.

"Do we want to get involved with them?"

"Not if we can help it. You know what it's like, they try to control everything. They're good at what they do, I'll give them that. If they get a lead, I'll take it. They don't know about you and Selena being on the scene. They won't have any reason to think it's more than a routine inquiry."

Stephanie came back into the room.

"That was quick. What have you got?"

"I talked with the chief up there. It's a small department. They don't have much. McCullough's friend worked for CDC down in Atlanta. The killer cut off an ear before he cut Campbell's throat."

"Only one reason to do that." Carter absently felt his ear. It was still attached to his head. "Torture. They wanted something from him."

"Cash and credit cards still in his wallet." Stephanie sat down. "His laptop is missing. No phone, either. Someone broke into the library where Campbell was working and got into the restricted archives. No one knows if anything is missing yet."

"No night watchman?"

"He drinks. He was asleep."

"Lucky for him, or he'd probably be dead. I think we can guess what's missing."

"The tablets." Harker thought for a moment. "Stephanie, bring up Campbell's phone logs. Let's see if he called anyone else. Maybe he sent that message to more than one person."

Steph went to a computer console off to the side of Harker's desk. The console fed into the big Crays downstairs. The Crays linked to the NSA database. Most messages sent over a cell phone or digital line were somewhere in that database. For sure all domestic messages. Campbell's calls would be there. Steph entered a string of commands.

"Got him. Several calls to Atlanta in the days before he was killed. Two a day to his home number. One long call to someone named Arnold Weinstein at CDC the day before he was killed. On the night of his murder, two calls. One to Kevin McCullough. Another to Weinstein. Those calls are back to back. Sent at 10:09 in the evening."

She began entering commands on her keyboard. "I'm checking on Weinstein now."

Nick tugged on his ear. "We need to talk with him."

"You'll need a hell of a connection." Steph stared at her monitor.

"What do you mean?"

"Weinstein got in his car to go to work this morning. It blew up when he turned on the ignition."

"A car bomb? Steph, can you retrieve the message from Campbell to Weinstein? Put it on the speakers."

"It will take a minute. Hold on." They waited. "All set."

They heard Campbell's voice. A voice from the grave.

"Arnold, it's James."
"Jim. Enjoying the weather up there? It was 78 here today."
"Arnie, I've got something." Campbell sounded excited.

"Oh?"

"I've been looking at records from Persia and I found something from the time of Alexander the Great. There was a devastating crop failure in Persia right after Xerxes the First returned from Greece. The famine that followed almost brought down his empire. These tablets I've been looking at might be a clue to the cause."

"Was there a draught?"

"That's what I thought at first. But water wasn't the problem. I think it was an unknown variant of Fusarium graminearum."

"Ah. That would do it."

"It's possible a store of Fusarium spores from then may have survived."

"You can't be serious." Weinstein sounded shocked.

"I am. One of the tablets describes a sealed vessel, an urn of gold. It's supposed to contain the curse of a goddess."

"Oh, come on, Jim. A curse?"

"Not a spell, something real. Xerxes brought it back with him from Greece around 490 BCE. I think it had spores in it, maybe from infected grains. It may even have been the cause of the famine. The Greeks could have isolated the cause without really understanding how it worked. They could have seen it as something to use against their enemies. The myth linked with the urn centers on the goddess of the harvest."

"You mean Demeter?"

"Yes. The urn was kept in the royal treasury. It was still there when Alexander defeated Darius III."

"What happened to it?"

"Alexander sent it back to Greece, along with the treasure."

"Then it's gone."

"What if it isn't? What if we could find it? This could be what the Pentagon has been asking for. If it is, I don't want to give it to them."

In Harker's office, they heard Weinstein sigh.

"Jim, this isn't a secured line."

"I don't give a damn. I didn't get into this field to turn science into a way to kill more people."

"Jim, please."

"If we can find this urn and it's what I think it is, we might come up with a way to wipe out Fusarium once and for all. Think of it, Arnie! New genetic material, uncontaminated. We have nothing that old to work with."

"It might not be different."

"No. But if it is..."

"How do you propose to find it? If it exists?"

"I think I know how, or at least how to begin."

"When are you coming back?"

"Tomorrow."

"Jim. Be careful."

"They wouldn't dare touch me, Arnie. You either. They need us. See you tomorrow."

The call ended.

"What's Fusarium whatever?" Nick asked.

"Let's find out." Steph's fingers moved over the keyboard. A picture came up. "It's a crop blight. Caused a lot of problems in the past. Spreads quickly, hard to stop, kills grains like wheat and barley. Reproduces with spores. Nasty stuff."

Elizabeth studied the picture on the screen. A field of wheat, rotten, black, spoiled.

"Campbell and Weinstein were working on something for the Pentagon and Campbell wasn't happy about it. They were virologists. It must be some kind of bio-weapon." She leaned back in her chair. "Campbell didn't seem to think he was in any real danger."

"Guess he was wrong about that," Nick said.

CHAPTER FOUR

Zviad Gelashvili sat sharpening a long steel blade he kept strapped low down on his left leg. He held it up to the light, inspected it, and continued the quiet stoke of the whetstone along the razor edge.

He was a huge man. His head came to a bald, round top under a workman's hat he wore to remind people of his peasant roots. He looked like a malevolent egg. He was known as "the egg". Not only because of his looks. Because anyone who annoyed or opposed him was turned into an unpleasant omelet.

The thick flesh of Zviad's face was marked by acne scars and jovial cruelty. He had a large nose and black eyes that glittered without warmth. His lips were large, tinged with purple. He was heavily muscled. The tailored shirts he wore cascaded forward over a mountainous gut balanced by huge buttocks that required special chairs to accommodate them. His shoes were of the finest leather, crafted by the most exclusive boot maker in London.

Gelashvili had risen to power in the criminal underworld of Moscow by emulating his idol and fellow Georgian, Iosif Vissarionovich Dzhugashvili, otherwise known as Stalin. If Zviad suspected treachery, someone died. If someone failed to carry out their assigned tasks, they died. If someone opposed him, they died. Something could always be done to encourage motivation.

Gelashvili was powerful and rich. He controlled part of Russia's energy deliveries to Germany and Western Europe. He controlled politicians, judges, police. He owned nightclubs and brothels in Moscow, Kiev and St. Petersburg.

Earlier in the day he'd gotten a phone call from a client he knew only as an anonymous voice over the phone. His accent was American and it was how Zviad thought of him, as "the American". Sometimes he'd hired Zviad to terminate someone, or wanted industrial secrets. Once he'd sought plans for one of the new fighters. It was all the same to

Zviad, as long as he was paid. The American always paid very well.

This time the client wanted Zviad to go to Greece, kidnap a woman and deliver her alive to a place where someone would take charge of her. A picture was faxed. The fee was generous. Zviad decided to send his younger brother to handle it. Bagrat was just as ruthless as he was. He could be trusted to do what was necessary.

Gelashvili lived in the heart of the city, just outside the Garden Ring and next to Gorky Park. He could see the park from the large French windows of his study. His wife had wanted something central, close in. He liked to indulge Bedisa. She rewarded him with sexual improvisation that made up for the inconvenience she represented. She'd disappointed him with two girls. Perhaps next time it would be a boy.

The gossip Bedisa heard in the posh salons and shops frequented by the wealthy women of Moscow often provided useful intelligence. She was shrewd. Overall, it was a good bargain. Zviad hoped she would never do something indiscreet. It would be a shame if the children lost their mother.

CHAPTER FIVE

The headquarters building of the Russian Foreign Intelligence Service, the *Sluzhba Vneshney Razvedki,* was in a part of the city very different from the neighborhood where Zviad Gelashvili contemplated the usefulness of his wife. There was no park across from SVR headquarters. People were not encouraged to loiter and feed the birds near the SVR building.

SVR was Russia's equivalent of the CIA, but operated with none of the restrictions that hampered Langley's operations. It carried on the old KGB tradition of espionage and assassination abroad. Not much ever changed about state security in Russia except names and technology. It had been that way in the days of the Czars. It would be that way tomorrow.

There were eight departments in the SVR. Deputy Director Alexei Ivanovich Vysotsky ran Department S, which included an Operations Department. The Operations Department in turn included an elite Special Operations Group known as Zaslon. Zaslon did not officially exist.

All Zaslon personnel were Spetsnaz, the best fighting men in Russia. Every member of Zaslon was trained for specialized foreign assignment and spoke at least three languages. Every member had demonstrated superior performance in a variety of secret military units. All had proved their courage under fire. They were fiercely loyal to the Rodina, the Motherland.

Zaslon was the sword of the Motherland. No enemies of Russia survived when Zaslon went looking for them.

Internal security within the Federation was handled by the FSB, the *Federal'naya Sluzhba Bezopasnosti,* headquartered at the old KGB headquarters in the Lubyanka east of Red Square. One area of friction between SVR and FSB concerned the growing power of the criminal gangs. The gang bosses controlled too much of Russia's wealth. Their wealth was manipulated from within the country, which made it FSB's problem. But gang operations extended far out into the world. As far as Eastern and Western Europe. As far as America. That made it Alexei's concern.

Sometimes carefully planned operations against the gangs went wrong, especially when operations concerned Zviad Gelashvili. General Vysotsky suspected a leak in the Lubyanka. Gelashvili was getting too powerful. He had become a danger to the Motherland. Alexei was determined to take him down.

Vysotsky was a genuine patriot. With the new administration things were changing. Alexei had high hopes. Hopes for a Russia reborn, without corrupt criminals shaping the future. A Russia respected and feared by the world.

Alexei was a handsome man in an elegant and menacing way, but he hadn't gotten where he was on good looks. Nor was it his ruthlessness. That went with his job. What had carried him to his position of power was instinct, a real sense for feeling out danger to the Motherland.

In his hands he held a report from an agent embedded deep in the American NSA. The report concerned the deaths of three scientists in America. As he read, the top of his skull tingled.

On the surface it didn't appear to be a security threat. Yet it was odd that all three were top researchers in the study of viruses. The report provided a translation of the cuneiform tablets and noted the possible connection to Alexander's treasure. It speculated that the killings might have been motivated by greed.

Not obviously a threat. Yet he had that tingle, that buzz of warning on the top of his head. Alexei always paid attention to that tingle. He decided to follow up on the report.

CHAPTER SIX

Afternoon sun poured over a set of glossy pictures spread out on the L-shaped kitchen countertop in Nick's apartment. The pictures were of a new luxury condo for sale near Du Pont Circle and the Convention Center in downtown D.C. A glass of Cabernet stood close by Selena's hand. Nick poured a fresh Irish whiskey. It was his third. He had a good buzz going.

Selena pointed at a photo. "The building has a great workout center. There's a pool on the roof. The price is good, too."

Nick read the price, discreetly printed near the bottom of the page. Seven figures, financing available. Three bedrooms, three baths, "well appointed kitchen", pantry and an enormous living room. The condo had a view that almost reached to the Rockies.

If Selena decided to buy it, she could write a check. It reminded Nick of the unbridgeable money gap between them. It hadn't come up much until now. The beautiful polished floors and sweeping views in the pictures made him feel his middle class roots to the bone.

"A bargain. Must be the lousy economy."

If Selena caught the irony in his tone she didn't show it.

"Now that I'm in D.C. all the time I thought I should get something permanent. Those rooms at the Mayflower are nice, but it's always been a temporary thing."

"What about your place in San Francisco?"

"Oh, I'll keep that. I love it. I'll pull a few of the art pieces and lease it out. I know someone who can handle that for me. I'm not using it now, but I don't want to let it go."

Some of the art pieces she referred to were priceless. One was a Paul Klee original. Nick supposed it would look as good in Washington as in San Francisco. He liked Paul Klee. He glanced at the reproduction Klee hanging over his couch. That one had cost ninety-nine dollars, ninety-five cents. Plus shipping.

"I think it's nice. I like the pool on the roof thing."

Selena picked up her glass, sipped. She watched him over the rim. "We could live there together."

"What's wrong with the way it is now?"

"We spend a lot of time running back and forth to each other's places. Why not make it simple? This is a beautiful place. It's near everything, it's got good security and it has a private garage. I get two parking spots."

Nick studied the view from the window. "It is nice. You should buy it if it's what you want."

"You don't want to live there with me." It wasn't a question. He heard the disappointment in her voice.

"It's not that."

"Then what is it?"

He turned to her. "It will change things between us. And it would always be your place."

"It would be our place. We can make it our place."

With two cats in the yard, he thought. A ghost of Megan. But Megan was gone. Why was he fighting the idea?

"I've got my habits. You have yours. You really think we can live together without messing it up?"

"We're never going to find out if we don't try."

Nick stared out the window. His own view wasn't bad. "It's not the habits, or whatever."

She waited.

"Look at what we do. God damn it, Selena, I'm afraid you'll get killed. Like Megan. I can't do that again."

"I'm not Megan."

"No, you're not." He stopped and started again. "When that bomb was going to go off, I thought how I hadn't told you how I felt."

She didn't have to ask which bomb. She wanted to ask him what he meant. She kept quiet.

God damn it, why was it so hard to say? What was he afraid of? If he said the words, things would change. He clenched the glass. Pain stabbed him behind his left eye. *The hell with it.*

"I love you, Selena. I haven't said that to anyone since Megan."

She froze, the wine glass half way to her lips. The words were an electric wave through her body. She realized she'd thought he'd never say it. Now he had.

"It took a bomb to make you say that? You haven't told me because you think I'll get killed?"

"Yes."

Selena set her glass down on the counter. "That's about the dumbest thing I've ever heard you say. What if you get killed? How do you think I'd feel about that?" She took a breath. "If we love each other, we should live together."

"So you love me."

"Nick. You are so fucking dense, sometimes."

She reached up and kissed him, a long, deep kiss. "Do you get it, now? Yes, I love you."

After a minute she backed away, her thoughts running into each other. One step at a time.

"What about this place?" She gestured at the pictures spread out on the counter.

Nick glanced at the pictures. Too many thoughts. "It's expensive."

Her uncle had been a very wealthy man and he'd left a lot of it to her. Nick never asked her about it. She never talked about it. She did now.

"I can afford it. Some of the money my uncle had went south with the economy. Some of it is tied up in the courts. The Chinese are being difficult about his investments over there. The rest is invested here. Half the interest goes to charity and I live on the other half. It's enough."

"It doesn't feel right. I'd have to pay my share."

"Does that mean you want to do this? Move in together?"

Nick felt a headache coming on. Maybe he ought to find out if it would work or it wouldn't.

"I'm not sure. Let me think about it."

"You don't have to be so enthusiastic."

He set his glass down and put his arms around her waist. "I can be enthusiastic."

The kiss tasted like wine. A few minutes later they were in the bedroom. The clothes came off and they fell on the bed. He kissed her, held her to him, felt the warmth of her, the beat of her heart, her breasts under his chest. He ran his fingers through her hair, over her body. She grasped his buttocks, squeezed.

"Nice," she whispered, her breath warm in his ear. He entered her.

They took a long time together. Somehow making love to her felt different. Maybe it had been the words.

CHAPTER SEVEN

Elizabeth Harker considered the implications of the murders. The killings were coordinated within 24 hours of each other. Only an organized group could pull off something like that.

The full team except for Lamont Cameron was assembled in her office. Lamont was at Bethesda undergoing a final check on his arm, shattered by a bullet in Khartoum months before.

Ronnie Peete was back from a week on the Navajo Reservation. He had on one of the Hawaiian shirts from his collection. This one was black, with white plumeria blossoms all over it. Subdued, for Ronnie.

Ronnie's skin was light brown with a hint of red. He had dark brown eyes that could spot a rabbit in the desert glare where others saw only rock and cactus. His tracking skills were legendary in Marine Recon. His large nose could have graced a bust from ancient Rome. Ronnie was broad shouldered, narrow hipped, 180 pounds of rock hard sinew and muscle.

Elizabeth picked up her pen.

"Selena, how are you coming with the translation?"

Selena wore a sleek tailored outfit of some green material that shimmered when she moved. The clothes looked comfortable. Harker wondered how she did it. Sometimes she felt a twinge of jealousy. *No one should look that good. I bet she can't cook*, she thought.

"It's done."

"And?"

"One part is a partial accounting of the treasury of Darius III. It mentions gold and silver coins, gold statues and the golden urn. The urn is supposed to contain the curse of the Greek goddess Demeter in her wrathful aspect. Alexander told someone called Aetolikos to escort the treasure back to Greece and return the urn to Demeter's temple. He gave him part of the treasure as a reward."

"Nice pay, if you can get it. A piece of the greatest treasure in history. What's the curse of Demeter?"

"That's spelled out in the other part. It's a fragment from a long epic of the period, a variation on the story of Persephone's descent to the underworld."

"Wait a minute." Nick interrupted. "Who's Persephone?"

Nick wore a light sport jacket of gray, a dark blue shirt and black slacks. No tie. Casual. He didn't look either casual or relaxed. He looked like he was wound tighter than spring steel, but he always looked like that. Elizabeth could tell by the way he moved that his back was hurting again. It had been that way on and off since the jump into Tibet.

"Persephone is Queen of the Dead, the daughter of Demeter. She was kidnapped and raped by Hades, king of the underworld. Sometimes she's linked with sexuality and war. The black horse on the urn was one of her symbols. It's where the word nightmare comes from."

"Sex and war, that figures. They kind of go together."

"You're hopeless." Selena shook her head. "There were a lot of bad consequences from the rape."

"Consequences?"

"Demeter is the goddess of the harvest and fertility. When she finds out Hades has taken her daughter, she goes into a rage. She shifts into her vengeful aspect as Demeter Erinys and makes everything stop reproducing. The crops die. There's famine, disease. No children. All the animals are sterile. She won't let anything grow or reproduce until Persephone is freed. One thing about Greek gods and goddesses, you didn't want to piss them off."

One of the things Nick liked about Selena was her earthy language. It wasn't something you expected from a background like hers.

"That's the curse?"

"Yes. She makes a deal with Zeus. In return for Persephone's freedom, she puts things back to normal and agrees not to do it again. All that is pretty standard. But in this version she hedges her bets. She hides her power to stop everything, just in case."

Ronnie said, "I'll bet I know where."

Selena waited.

"In a golden urn."

"That's right."

Harker picked up the silver pen that had belonged to FDR. She began tapping. Thinking.

"Sometimes there's a historical basis for these stories, something real. I wonder if there's something behind this one?"

"Campbell thought there was," Nick said.

"Campbell, Weinstein and McCullough had two things in common. They knew about the story on the tablets and they were experts in the same field. Campbell and Weinstein also had high security clearances."

"Why would they need high clearances?" Selena asked.

"They were working on something secret for the Pentagon," Elizabeth said. "It wouldn't be the first time CDC was involved in a bio-warfare program."

"The Greeks used bio-warfare. They'd throw dead plague victims over the walls of a besieged city, or catapult poisonous snakes onto enemy ships. Poison the water supply with dead animals."

"Never seems like there's anything really new, does it?" Harker rolled her pen around on her desk. "Campbell thought the urn was important. But we don't know what happened to it."

"We know Alexander gave it to Aetolikos," Selena said. "I followed up on him. He turns out to be a cousin of Alexander, one of his sub-commanders. Family."

"Did you find out where he took it?"

"He dropped off the treasure in Pella and went home to Dion. There's no record of him after that. Dion was in Macedonia and had a big temple dedicated to Demeter. It was overrun when the Persians invaded. That might be where Xerxes found the urn."

"You think Alexander's cousin took it back to Dion?"

"It makes sense. He would have seen it as returning something of the goddess to it's rightful place."

"It doesn't seem likely it would still be around," Nick said.

Selena shrugged. "No. But the town is still there."

"We have to try and find out what happened to that urn." Harker turned to Selena. "How's your Greek?"

CHAPTER EIGHT

The hotel bed was uncomfortable. The room was stuffy, the red drapes on the windows dark and heavy. The thick smog of Athens made her eyes water. She was glad when her plane lifted off and she left the city behind.

Dion was a long way north of Athens, at the foot of Mount Olympus. The nearest airport was Thessaloniki. At Thessaloniki Selena rented a car and wound her way 70 kilometers north to her next hotel. The desk clerk was eager to please. Guests were few, even at this five star resort. The beautiful beach outside her hotel window was almost deserted. A man strolled with his dog. A young couple huddled under a shared blanket against a steady breeze coming off the Aegean.

Her first solo assignment. *You're not in Kansas, anymore,* she thought to herself. *You're on your own.* It felt good. It also felt a little scary, without the team around her.

She wasn't armed. This was just a research trip, no different from trips she'd taken in the past to research some point of language or culture. She didn't expect trouble, but Nick's words echoed in her head.

Never think things are what they appear to be. Always watch for the false word, the hidden knife, the gun. Trust no one.

Trust no one.

It wasn't a new thought. It had taken a long time to trust again after her parents and brother died. She'd been ten years old. Then she'd grown into an attractive woman and learned not to trust men. She still didn't trust most of them. Nick was an exception. She'd trust him with her life, that wasn't a problem. Trusting him with her heart, that was another matter. He'd said he loved her. She knew he meant it, in his own way, but that didn't mean it was trustworthy. There were a lot of different levels of trust. She brushed the confusing thoughts aside and considered her mission.

Aetolikos had come home a long time ago. He was related to Alexander, he'd been important. Something might have turned up about him during excavations in the area. The archeological museum in Dion was the best place to start. If that didn't work out, she'd ask around the village. There could be something in local oral traditions.

The hotel restaurant smelled of the sea. It was large and almost empty. She ordered dolmades, a salad, a bottle of mineral water, some bread and oil. A middle-aged man read a newspaper over coffee at a corner table. Four older couples, probably from a tour, sat near the windows looking bored.

Two large men in boxy, dark suits came in and sat down. They glanced her way, then ignored her. They ordered lunch in stilted English, along with a bottle of retsina, the strong Greek drink she thought tasted like turpentine. They began talking business. It took her a moment to place the language as Georgian. Selena couldn't speak it, but she understood the basics. From what she could make out, the men were talking about importing olives. Or maybe they were selling them.

Selena tuned them out and ate her meal slowly, thinking about Nick and what it would be like to live with him. Maybe it would be better to leave things as they were. She finished, signed her bill and walked past the table with the two men. Their eyes followed her out of the room.

It was Saturday, already after noon, and the museum closed at 2:30 on Saturday during the winter months. She decided to go now. She got directions to the museum at the desk.

The day was beautiful and chill, with the clear blue sky and crystalline quality of sunlight she'd found nowhere in the world except Greece. For Selena, it was one of the most beautiful and interesting places in the world. Snow-capped Mount Olympus dominated the spectacular scenery.

Olympus, the home of the gods. She wondered what the gods would think of modern Greece, mired in a sea of opportunistic corruption and impossible debt. Even Ulysses would not have been able to sail those waters.

The museum was modern, two stories high. She paid a modest fee and began exploring. The first floor was given

32

over to artifacts and sculpture. A nice statue of Dionysius, god of wine. A display featuring coins and relics from early Christian and Roman sites in the area. Interesting, but none of it useful. She went upstairs.

The prime exhibit was a hydraulic water organ over two thousand years old. She wondered what the music had sounded like. The rest of the floor dealt with life in classical Dion. Tools. Pottery. A child's toy horse, small statues of the gods, everything displayed in glass cases that ran along the walls or stood on plinths on their own.

Selena came to a new section. The centerpiece of the display was a full scale cast taken from the lid of a tomb. It was perfect, unmarred by weather and time. A young and handsome face was carved on the lid in bas relief, helmeted and confident and haughty, the lips full and voluptuous. Even in the cold white of plaster the face was astounding, beautiful, perfectly proportioned, as if the lips would suddenly open and speak. Selena looked at the inscription engraved below and translated in her mind.

Aetolikos
Safe in Elysium

CHAPTER NINE

"You found his tomb?"

Harker put Selena's call on the speaker. Nick and Stephanie listened.

"Not his tomb. A cast taken from inside it. The tomb was only discovered last fall. The archeologist in charge sealed it and stopped excavation during the winter rains, but he's about to start up again."

"How did you find that out?"

"I had coffee with the curator of the museum. He was thrilled to have someone to talk to and very enthusiastic about the tomb. It's built into the side of a hill with several rooms. The connection to Alexander makes it a priority dig. There could be something there."

"Can you get into it?"

"I don't know. I've got some names and I've got the location. Nothing's going to happen until Monday."

"What's your plan?"

"Go out there, introduce myself, use my credentials. Butter up the chief archeologist and hint at good publicity for him. Everyone wants academic recognition. Tell him I'd appreciate a guided tour. I think he'll go for it."

"And?"

"If I see something, check it out."

Harker picked up her pen, twirled it in her fingers. Nick waited for the tapping to begin and breathed an inward sigh of relief when she set it down.

"Is anyone else showing interest?"

"Not that I've noticed." The connection hissed with atmospherics. "This place is like a ghost town. There aren't many people staying here. The ones I've seen don't strike me as unusual. A couple of businessmen from Georgia. A couple of honeymooners. Some older folks."

"What are American businessmen doing in Dion?" Nick asked. His ear began itching.

"Not Georgia like Atlanta. Georgia as in the nation. I didn't pay much attention. They were talking over lunch, something about exporting olives to Russia."

Someone knocked on her door.

"Just a minute." She called out. "Yes?"

"Room service." The voice was muffled.

Still holding the phone, she walked to the door. "Room service. I didn't order anything. Hang on."

She started to open the door. It slammed into her, knocking her back into the room. The phone flew from her hand. The two men she had seen in the restaurant came hard into the room.

Twenty years of martial arts kicked in. Master Kim had seen promise in his young student and taken her aside for special instruction. Over the years he'd taught her a more dangerous level of the art.

She'd landed on her back on the floor when the men burst in. Selena used the movement to somersault herself back and up. She stepped to the side of the man charging at her, grabbed his jacket with both hands and brushed him with her hip. His momentum sent him flying into the wall across the room. The second was on her, wrapping his arms around her. She knew better than to try and use her strength to escape. Instead, she spit in his face. He pulled back in reflex. She head butted him with everything she had. He wasn't expecting it and loosed his hold.

It was enough. She pivoted and used her left hand to grasp his right in a wrist lock and bore down. The hard lock sent an instant, overwhelming pain up his arm. It blocked thought for a critical instant, all she needed. She reached under his elbow with her other hand and levered the elbow up and in and away. It made an ugly sound like a wet branch breaking. He screamed in agony. She moved back and kicked him in the groin with her leg and heel extended, crushing his testicles. He screamed again and fell to the floor.

The other man had a gun, a big automatic. She spun with a high kick and knocked it from his hand. She followed with a strike to the solar plexus, a blow to the throat, a deadly fist up under the ribcage. He collapsed. His face went purple. He died.

The first attacker moaned in pain, clutching his groin. His right arm lay at an odd angle. Selena walked over to him. She felt cold, her mind clear and focused. He had touched her, grabbed her. He had wanted to hurt her, worse, she had no doubt. She considered the strike that would kill him. Just in time, she thought better of it. He would have answers.

She shivered. Where did this urge to kill come from? What had happened to her civilized education, her deep sense of compassion, her sense of common humanity? For an instant they'd vanished like a wisp of smoke in a harsh wind.

It was the Project. Since she'd joined the Project, things has changed. For years she'd hidden behind a comfortable veneer of academic and athletic achievement. She'd had control of her life, everything neatly organized. That was gone. Life in the Project had stripped it away.

She didn't know where this new life was taking her.

Selena bent over the sobbing man as he tried to crawl away from her. She placed her thumb on a nerve center and pressed until he was unconscious. An act of mercy, really, and now it was quiet in the room. Somewhere in the background she heard her name, a tinny voice far away.

The phone. It lay on the rug where it had fallen. She walked over, bent down and picked it up. She was breathing hard. Her forehead hurt. A trickle of blood ran from her nose. She wiped it away with her knuckle.

Nick was shouting. "Selena!"

"It's all right." She walked over to the dead man. "I guess the olive business isn't what it used to be."

CHAPTER TEN

Nick touched down in Thessaloniki sixteen hours after Selena's call. The flight was official, cleared with the Greeks. Nick wasn't pretending to be someone he wasn't. He'd brought a Glock .40 for Selena. His own H-K rested in the shoulder rig under his jacket.

It was Sunday morning when he arrived. The sky was cloudy with patches of sun through scudding clouds. He smelled rain coming.

A white police car with blue stripes waited outside the hotel entrance. A bored constable stood by the car smoking a cigarette. He watched Nick enter the hotel.

Selena opened her door. Her forehead was red and swollen, her violet eyes red-rimmed with fatigue. She smiled. He felt something jump inside him. Behind her, a small, dark man stood near the window.

"You okay?"

She nodded. "Nick, this is Chief Inspector Giorgos Demetrios from the police. We were just talking."

She made the introduction.

Demetrios was around five-seven, maybe 140 pounds. He wore civilian clothes, a brown suit of indifferent cut. His shoes were black and dull. His tie had stains on it. His hair was short and curly, showing gray. He had a paunch and needed a shave. Nick guessed him at around fifty-five years old. Dark eyes watched them with the calculating gaze universal to cops everywhere. He looked annoyed. Demetrios had a Smith and Wesson 910 holstered on his belt.

Chief Inspector. At his age, that wasn't much. He was stuck at the equivalent of a first lieutenant in the military, a working cop. Demetrios wasn't going any higher up the promotion ladder.

Selena had killed one of the attackers. It could complicate things.

"Carter." Demetrios spoke passable English. "I recognize you. From the films of Jerusalem, with your President."

Damn, Nick thought, *the Jerusalem thing again.* It had compromised him, blown his cover in a big way. Every agency in the world had his picture.

Demetrios didn't waste words. "I want to know why you are here and why Doctor Connor was attacked. And why you are armed." He gestured at the bulge under Nick's gray jacket. "Foreigners are not allowed to carry guns here. Not without official permission."

"I have permission, Chief Inspector. Selena and I work for our government as a kind of floating investigative team. We look into things that might be against the country's interests. In this case, international interests, including those of Greece."

They needed as much help as they could get. Nick decided to tell Demetrios most of it, except about the golden urn. This cop could make a lot of trouble for them if he wanted to. It would delay things.

"We think this incident is related to three murders in the US. It involves historical artifacts."

"Artifacts?"

"Treasure from the days of Alexander. He sent it back from Persia."

"And your investigation brought you here, to Macedonia."

"Yes."

He gave Selena a speculative look. "The man you killed had your picture in his pocket. I received bulletins from Interpol last night. The criminals who attacked you are members of a powerful gang based in Moscow. Why would these people have your photograph?"

Chief Inspector Demetrios walked over to the window and studied the view. "They must believe you have a way to find this missing treasure. If there is any. How much are we talking about?" His voice was casual.

"We don't know," Nick said. "Maybe a lot. One of Alexander's cousins may have brought part of it here, to Dion. I doubt it still exists. But someone must think it does."

"Any items related to Alexander would be of the highest historical importance to my country. I insist that you share any information you have with me." Demetrios' voice had taken on an authoritative edge.

Nick held up his hands. "We need your help, Chief Inspector. We're not treasure hunters, we're investigators. We want the people behind those murders, nothing else."

He could see Demetrios thinking. Uncovering relics of Alexander might salvage his career. Self-motivation made for good allies. Greed was also a good motivation. Nick suspected Demetrios was thinking as much about gold as his country's history.

Selena told him about the tomb. Demetrios agreed to arrange a look at the tomb on Monday. He opened the door and paused.

"Let me be clear about something, Carter. I am in charge, here. You will not act on your own. " His tone was hostile. "You are foreigners in my country. I will investigate why you have permission to carry weapons. You will not leave the hotel without escort. You will not take any action without my express permission. Do you understand?"

"Perfectly." So much for making allies. Maybe he needed to brush up on his diplomatic skills.

Demetrios went out. The door closed behind him.

"Nice to get a warm welcome," Nick said.

"What the hell were those thugs doing with my picture?" The words spurted out. Selena paced across the room and back again. She was upset.

"We'll find out. Let's go down to the restaurant. No point in trying to think on an empty stomach."

"You're impossible."

"You've said that before. Always eat when you can. You don't know when the next time will be."

"Is that another one of your damned rules?"

"Come on, we'll talk about it over coffee."

In the dining room Nick told Selena what Harker had learned about the men who'd attacked her.

"They came up on Interpol right away. They belong to a gang in Russia."

"The Russian Mafia?"

"Similar. There are about fifteen powerful gangs in Russia. This one is Georgian. The outfit is run by a man named Zviad Gelashvili. The man you kicked in the balls is his brother, Bagrat Gelashvili. Along with the Ukrainians, the Georgians are the worst. That's saying a lot."

"His brother? Why would a crime boss send his brother after me? Why here?"

"Gelashvili must know about the tablets. He's probably after Alexander's treasure. He sent those goons to follow up on the same trail we're looking at. That doesn't tell us how he found out about it in the first place."

"How could they know who I am?"

"Someone sent him who knows who you are and what you're doing here. It has to be someone who knows about the Project. Plus they have to be able to get someone on the scene here the same day you arrive. That means first rate organization and intel. It could be an Agency. CIA, DIA, someone like that."

She sighed and pushed her plate away. "Nothing is ever simple in this job, is it?"

CHAPTER ELEVEN

"Come."

The man who entered Alexei Ivanovich Vysotsky's office was tall. He wore a dark blue suit. He moved with contained energy, like a controlled explosion. He was handsome in a hard way, with blond hair cropped close to his skull. A small enameled flag of the Russian Federation gleamed on his jacket lapel. There was a small scar on his chin.

His eyes were cold blue, the eyes of a man who knew what he was and was afraid of nothing. He had the kind of military look found on recruiting posters. A hint of reddish shadow colored his jaw. His name was Arkady Korov.

He was dedicated and intelligent and lethal, everything an officer of Zaslon was supposed to be. If you wanted a robot there were plenty who could fill that role, but Korov wasn't one of them. He was perfect for the job Alexei had in mind. Korov reached the desk and snapped to attention. Vysotsky carried the rank of Major General.

"At ease, Major." Alexei gestured at a chair in front of the desk.

Korov sat. Alexei handed him an Interpol report of an incident in Greece involving an American woman and Georgian criminals. Interpol thought it was a foiled attempt at kidnapping and ransom. The report stated the woman was wealthy. She was. It didn't mention the Project, but Alexei was aware of Selena's real role.

"What do you think of this?"

Korov scanned the document. "Zviad's brother, Bagrat. This seems to be a kidnapping that went wrong."

"You find nothing odd?"

"Several things. Why Greece or kidnapping? It doesn't fit Gelashvili's pattern. It says one died and Bagrat is seriously injured. How would a woman defeat these men? Bagrat is as bad as his brother. He's an animal, very strong."

Alexei was pleased. "Exactly. The woman is not what she appears to be. She is part of an elite American intelligence group."

Korov raised an eyebrow. "What is she doing in Greece?"

"Looking for treasure. Or perhaps something else."

"Treasure?"

"She is following a trail that has been cold for a very long time." Alexei told Korov about the tablets and murder of three prominent American virologists.

"What will happen now that Gelashvili failed?"

"That is what you are going to find out, Arkady."

Korov noted the use of his first name. It told him this assignment was important. Vysotsky opened a desk drawer, took out a bottle of vodka and two glasses. He poured.

"Na Z'drovnya." To your health. The men drank.

"I need more information. That is where you come in."

"Why are the Americans involved?"

"I don't know. This group is not like other American intelligence units. They are mobile and unrestricted, much as we are. If they're pursuing this there is fire behind the smoke. It is a complication, no more. My concern is Gelashvili. If the Americans bring him down, so much the better. Who knows, perhaps they will help you. Maybe you should look them up and introduce yourself."

Korov didn't smile.

"It's a joke, Major. But in this case, there may be a common goal."

Korov waited.

Alexei thought for a moment. "I think Bagrat Gelashvili will suffer complications from his injuries, even fatal ones."

Korov nodded. He didn't need to ask how that might be accomplished while Bagrat was in police custody. It would be up to him to arrange the details.

"You will proceed at once to Greece." Alexei handed Korov a packet. "You leave at 15:30 hours. This contains your legend, tickets, passport, money, driver's license and

Bagrat's present location. Our contact in Athens will provide any weapons and supplies you require. Take care of Bagrat. Investigate. Find out anything you can about the Americans. You have full freedom to pursue your mission in any way you think fit."

Korov knew if anything went wrong, he would be blamed. On the other hand, he had all the freedom he needed to succeed. He smiled.

CHAPTER TWELVE

Arkady's flight landed on time. He took a room in the Plaka, the neighborhood below the Acropolis. His contact ran a shop here that catered to the tourist trade. There were always tourists in Athens. Arkady's passport identified him as Wilhelm Wimmer, a German architect on holiday. No one would think it unusual for an architect to visit Greece. Classical Greek architecture was still admired around the world.

Arkady found satisfaction in buildings like the Acropolis. The neat rows of columns, the perfect proportions, the folly of humans reflected in the actions of their gods. Korov had a genuine appreciation of history and Greek culture. He considered himself an educated man, though most of his education had been in the art of war.

The Russian adventure in Afghanistan was over by the time Arkady received his commission as a Junior Lieutenant. There was no shortage of other conflicts. He'd been recruited into Spetsnaz while serving in Chechnya. After that, things got interesting. Counter-terrorism in Tadzhikistan and Uzbekistan against the Islamic militant subversives. Special Advisor duty in Syria. He'd never married and everyone else was gone. His unit was his only family.

It was night in Athens. The Acropolis was bathed in light on the hill above his window. Tomorrow he would get his weapons and rent a car to drive north. Bagrat Gelashvili was being held under close guard at a hospital in Thessaloniki. His injuries were severe.

They were going to get worse.

CHAPTER THIRTEEN

Monday morning felt gray and damp with the raw smell of spring. Low walls of weathered stone wandered over ancient fields near the tomb. The land was green with fresh grass, sprinkled with white and blue wildflowers. Mount Olympus loomed in the background, shrouded in dark clouds. If the gods were home, no one cared.

The entrance to the tomb yawned in the side of a large hill. Centuries of overgrowth had been pushed aside to expose a rectangular stone opening. A silent diesel generator sat by the entrance. Cables on the ground coiled into the tomb like Medusa's snakes.

Nick assumed the generator and cables were for lighting. That was good. He'd had enough of dark tunnels and enclosed spaces for a lifetime. Tombs didn't bother him. The shades of the dead didn't bother him, except in his dreams. But lightless caves and tunnels, that was another story.

He stood with Selena, Demetrios and Abraxas Papadakis, the archeologist in charge of excavating the tomb. Demetrios hadn't spoken to them since he'd arrived. A group of workmen lounged nearby, smoking and talking, waiting for someone to tell them what to do. They didn't seem in any hurry.

Papadakis was a round, muscular man. He wore clear bifocals attached to a band behind uneven ears that stuck out from the side of his head. His face was lined from years spent working outdoors. His teeth were bad.

Selena chatted away in Greek with Papadakis. Demetrios scowled. Papadakis was entranced.

"They plan to open the rear chamber today," Selena said. "Our timing couldn't be better. It's the last place to explore in the tomb."

Papadakis switched to English for Nick's benefit. "Doctor Connor is right, good timing. The Romans looted these sites but missed this one. We cleared the front before the winter and now we're opening the back. It shouldn't take long to clear the debris blocking the entrance to the rear chamber."

He was excited. "Let's begin, shall we?"

He barked out orders to the workmen. One man started the generator. The noise shattered the spring morning. A flock of birds rose in fright from a nearby tree. The workers picked up their tools and disappeared into the entrance.

Nick followed the archeologist, Demetrios and Selena through the low doorway. Inside, the ceiling was high enough to stand upright. It was cold and damp. Bright lights threw a flickering glare over walls faced with white marble. Empty niches were carved into the walls at regular intervals. A rectangular marble box held place of honor in the center of the tomb. It was simple in design, about three feet high. On the lid was the bas relief and inscription Selena had seen in the museum.

The last stop for Aetolikos, sub-commander, cousin of Alexander the Great. Papadakis answered their unasked question.

"He's still in there. We found two gold coins from Persia inside his skull. They'd been placed on his eyes to pay the boatman."

"The boatman?" Nick asked.

"Charon. He ferried souls across the River Styx to the underworld. You had to give him his fare or you'd be stranded on this side forever. An unpleasant fate."

"Wouldn't do to be broke when you died, I guess." Nick placed his hand on the marble coffin.

Aetolikos had ridden with Alexander the Great against the King of Persia. He'd watched the war banners streaming in the wind under the Persian sky. He'd seen the bright swords and long spears glinting in the sun, heard the clash of battle. He'd smelled the dust and blood. He'd heard the screams of slaughtered men and animals.

Nick knew what the dust and blood of battle smelled like, had followed the sounds of war for days and months on end. For Aetolikos, in an age that honored heroes, they were days of glory. For Nick, in an age that forgot its heroes, they were days of bad memories and worse dreams.

He felt depressed. A warrior's life, reduced to a box of dried bones with strangers picking coins from his skull. Everyone ended up in the same place.

Papadakis stood at the back of the room and watched the workmen. The passage was narrow. The men passed debris back in a chain and placed it to the side. There was a shout from the front of the line.

"They've broken through," Selena said.

They waited for the workmen to back out. Papadakis picked up a strong electric torch. He would be first into the chamber. Nick, Selena and Demetrios crowded close behind. They crawled through the opening and stood inside the final room.

The chamber was large and empty. A niche had been carved into the rock on the back wall. An image of a horse had been cut into the wall above. There were still traces of black pigment on the stone. Beside it, letters were roughly chiseled into the wall, as if someone had been in a hurry when they carved it.

Papadakis shone his light on the inscription. Selena read over his shoulder. The archeologist sighed.

Erinys waits for you
By the springs of Thrace
Where the two rivers cross
Seek her and die

"It's a message." he translated for Nick's benefit.

"Erinys?" He remembered what Selena had said back in Virginia. "Demeter in her vengeful aspect?"

Papadakis nodded in approval. "That's right. The black horse is the symbol of Persephone. A night mare. You know Persephone?"

"I can't keep all these names straight. Persephone, Demeter, Erinys. The same goddess, right?"

Papadakis smiled. "Not exactly, although some see it that way."

He turned back to the inscription. "This is a taunt to the Romans. Probably written around 147 or 146 BCE during the final conquest of Greece. The legions were pillaging as they came. If something was here then it was taken away and hidden."

He swept his hand around the room. "I've never seen anything like this before. It's completely atypical."

The walls were unmarked except for the inscription, the horse and the empty niche. The room was plain, cut from the living rock. It was more like a storage room than a tomb.

"It looks like a riddle." Selena ran her fingers along the chiseled letters.

"I doubt that. Just typical poetic expression. It probably means the locals fled into Thrace and if the Romans came after them, they'd be killed. But Thrace already had large Roman settlements. Classic bravado. It's what finally got Rome annoyed enough to turn Greece into provinces."

"Where is Thrace?" Nick looked at the inscription.

"Modern day Bulgaria. The old Thrace ended at the Balkan Mountains to the north and included Western Turkey, this side of the Bosporus."

"Maybe whatever was here was taken to Thrace."

Papadakis shrugged. "We'll never know. But this is interesting. It will make for several good papers." He peered at the inscription.

The academic mind at work. Nick saw Selena smile and look at him. They made their way out of the tomb, back to the outside world. A light rain drifted over the grass and trees. The earth smelled rich and full. After the tomb it felt like a return to life. The drops made minute explosions against his skin.

Papadakis had stayed inside. Demetrios stood with Nick and Selena in the rain. He pulled up the collar of his coat.

"I'm wondering about that inscription, " Nick said.

"Yes?" Demetrios gave him a hostile look.

"I think Selena is right and our archeologist may be wrong. I think it's a riddle, or some kind of message. More than a jab at the Romans."

"You think it is a message about the treasure?"

"It could be."

Selena wiped a few drops of water from her face. They began walking to the cars.

"You heard Papadakis, Chief Inspector. The room isn't typical. Something was there. Why else build it like that?"

"You are both speculating. We know nothing about what was in that room."

"But we know someone left a message there. It's the only clue we've got. I think we have to pursue it."

Demetrios stood by the side of his car. "I'm going to Thessaloniki to interrogate Gelashvili."

"We should go with you."

"No, Carter, you should not. You will remain here until I return."

Selena knew Nick was getting ready to blow. She touched his arm "We'll be here. I want to use the internet at the hotel."

"I will return tomorrow. You are restricted to the hotel." Demetrios got in the police car and drove away.

Nick shook his head as the car left them behind. "What an asshole."

"An unpleasant man. Never mind him. That niche was about the right size for something two cubits high."

"I was thinking the same thing."

"Let's go back to the hotel."

Neither noticed the old man standing in a grove of olive trees not far from the tomb. The man had the look of someone who had worked at hard labor in the fields all his life. He was dark and stooped. He wore a cloth workman's hat. He watched the car with the two foreigners grow smaller until it turned out of sight. He sighed, crossed himself and shuffled away in the rain.

CHAPTER FOURTEEN

Thessaloniki was a big city. There were ruins, fortifications, sites of ancient battles. Korov thought he'd look around and explore after his business with Gelashvili.

Gelashvili was under guard in the AHEPA University hospital. It was a modern complex with several wings and outlying structures. Korov parked near the main entrance. The day was gray with steady, soaking rain. He went over the steps of penetration in his mind.

Korov had studied plans of the building. He knew where the stairways were located, where the roof exits were, how many elevators there were and where they went, where the various departments were situated.

He'd chosen one of his favorite weapons for this assignment. The PSS Silent Pistol fired a 7.62X41mm armor piercing round. The unique design prevented escape of any explosive gases. Gases made noise. It had the additional advantage of short barrel length and small size. The pistol was ideal for his purpose. Conventionally silenced pistols were incredibly loud compared to the PSS. No one would hear more than a light cough when it was fired. It only held six rounds, but that wasn't a problem. He wouldn't need six.

Gelashvili would be restrained in his bed with handcuffs to the frame. There would be a guard outside his door. If there were two guards, things could get messy. Probably, only one.

Korov had another Spetsnaz favorite with him, an OC23 Drotik. The Drotik fired a small 5.45X18mm round from a magazine of 26. He could select single, three round or full auto fire. At 1800 rounds per minute, the pistol was uniquely lethal. It had light recoil, easily controlled.

He got out of the car and walked to the entrance. A semi-circle of flags set on tall poles hung like wet sheets in the rain. A long portico extended over the main doors. He walked inside. Leaping figures were painted on the walls against a yellow background. Korov supposed it was meant to convey a sense of health and energy. He straightened his tie and walked to the information desk. A middle-aged woman sat behind the counter, entering data on a computer. She glanced up as he approached.

"Excuse me," Korov said in English. Anyone behind that desk would have to speak English. He took out his wallet and showed her identification stating he was Inspector Allon Dubois of Interpol. He was wearing a dark suit of European cut, the kind of suit an international cop might wear.

"I am here to interview a prisoner, Gelashvili. Can you tell me where he is?"

Korov held the ID close so she could read it. It would have gotten him into Interpol HQ. The forgers at SVR were the best in the world. It was a source of comfort to agents in the field.

"One moment, Inspector." She entered a few keystrokes. "He's in 4003. Fourth floor." She pointed. "Take the elevator down the hall. On the fourth floor, turn left, go to the second corridor, turn right and you'll see it on the left."

"Thank you. You've been very helpful." He smiled at her and turned to the elevators.

"Your colleagues are already here."

"Oh?" Korov turned back. "Both of them?"

"Yes, about a half hour ago. Shall I call up and let them know you're coming?"

"No, thank you. I'll just go on up. They knew I'd be late."

He walked away toward the elevators. He glanced back at the helpful clerk. She'd gone back to her computer. Good. No phone call. He had to make a choice. Abort and try again later? What if the agents were here to move Gelashvili to a secure location? He couldn't take the chance.

He might need the Drotik after all.

CHAPTER FIFTEEN

Outside Nick and Selena's hotel the wind had picked up. Nick stood in front of the windows looking out. The drizzle had changed into hard rain. The Aegean Sea was almost invisible through the sheets of water pounding against the window. Somewhere across the waters lay Homer's Troy. He could hear heavy surf driving up against the shore below. Selena sat in an armchair with her laptop. She'd been sitting there for the last hour.

Nick was beginning to think they were at a dead end, caught up in a wild goose chase. The chances of finding the urn or any part of Alexander's treasure were slim to none. How long could something like that remain hidden? This was Europe, plundered and pillaged and raped by armies, jacked up kings and brutal emperors for thousands of years. No one could conceal that kind of wealth for all those centuries. Then again, no one had ever found the Templar treasure. Maybe it was possible.

He watched Selena. Her face was a study in concentration. He thought about the condo in D.C. and moving in together. He had no clarity in his thoughts about it. The lease on his apartment didn't run out for another year. He decided he'd hold onto it for now.

"Look at this." Selena broke into his thoughts. He went over to the screen. It showed a tourist portal for Bulgaria.

"Bulgaria."

"Yes. Or Thrace, if you prefer."

"What did you find?"

"I went looking for something to match that inscription. Remember? 'By the springs of Thrace, where the two rivers cross.' I think I know the general area. There are a lot of springs in Bulgaria."

She moved the mouse, clicked. A picture appeared on the screen of a large city with big churches, cobbled streets and happy people. The churches were dome shaped and old. The people were young. None of them were dome shaped.

"Sofia?"

"It's Sofia, accent on the first syllable. The capitol of Bulgaria. It was settled in the seventh century BCE and built around a mineral spring."

"What about the rivers?"

"Sofia sits in a big valley at the foot of a mountain. There are two rivers that run through the city, the Vladaiska and the Perlovska."

"Two rivers crossing and a spring. I think you got it. But we're going to need more than that. It still doesn't pinpoint an exact location."

"It's all we've got. The inscription might have been left for someone besides the Romans."

"Someone who needed to know where the treasure was taken."

"Yes." She stretched.

"Doesn't mean it's still there or we can find it."

"No, but we're a step closer if I'm right. Maybe we could smoke out someone with this."

"How do you mean?"

"We could let the idea about Sofia slip out. Maybe someone turns up where they shouldn't and we can track them back to the source."

"And pin it down." He thought about it. "It's a good idea. We'll run it by Harker. She can decide how to do it."

She stood and walked to the window. It was still raining. The wind had died. The sea was gray and uninviting. She thought about Homer's description of the Aegean as the "wine dark sea". It was dark, all right, but it wasn't the color of wine today.

Nick came up behind her. "What's going on with Steph?"

"What do you mean?"

"She seems different somehow. Lighter."

"You really don't know?"

"Know what?"

"She's sleeping with Lucas. I think she's in love with him."

"You're kidding. He's CIA."

"What difference does it make?"

"Security comes to mind. Plus he works for Lodge."

"Lucas has high security clearance. And he doesn't work for Lodge, he works for Hood. Steph isn't going to tell him anything. I don't think he'd talk to her, either."

"Harker know about this?"

"I'd be amazed if she didn't. She hasn't said anything. Steph deserves to be with someone if she wants. It's not easy in our work. "

"Tell me about it."

"Are you hungry?"

"Yes." He reached for her and drew her close. He slipped his hand down inside the back of her skirt. "I'm hungry. For you."

"Me too."

They undressed each other. She ran her hands down his right side, down his leg, feeling over ridges and welts of scar tissue left by the grenade. She touched the puckered scar where a round had gone through his shoulder.

"You should duck more," she said.

"Don't have to, when I'm lying down."

It wasn't long before neither one of them was standing.

CHAPTER SIXTEEN

Korov stepped from the elevator and turned left. Ahead he spotted two orderlies and a doctor. in blue scrubs talking with an elderly couple. Two more men in white coats and stethoscopes, interns or doctors. The nurse's station was about fifty feet from the elevators. An exit sign marked the stairs at the end of the main corridor.

The place smelled like every hospital he'd ever been in, of antiseptic and worry and illness and efficiency. The floors were polished and clean, light colored, synthetic. The air was too warm.

He passed a set of swinging doors emblazoned with red and yellow radiation signs and warnings in Greek, English and French. Two men and a woman in green came through the doors talking. They ignored him and walked by. He started past the nurse's station.

"Sir."

It was the nurse on duty.

Korov showed his Interpol ID. "I'm going to 4003."

He kept walking. The nurse started to say something. Her phone buzzed. She picked it up. Korov continued down the hall. As he came to the second intersecting corridor he slowed. Ahead, the hallway was empty except for a gurney standing against one wall. He reached the intersection and glanced quickly to the right. A bored policeman sat in a plastic chair outside one of the rooms.

That's it. One cop. The others must still be inside.

In his mind, Korov pictured how the room would be. The bed would be to the left or right, it made no difference. There would be a bathroom on the other side. The bed might have a curtain. If the curtain was open, no problem. If the curtain was closed, it could be a problem. It could slow him down.

Korov eased the PSS from his holster and palmed it in his hand. In his other he held the false ID. He walked up to the cop, the ID displayed in front. As the cop read the ID

Korov shot him in the chest. He slumped forward. The noise was no more than a gentle sneeze. In Korov's mind, a clock began ticking down.

Arkady reached out and settled the corpse upright in the chair. Anyone looking down the hall would see a policemen sitting on duty. It would do for the next two minutes. That was all Arkady needed. If anyone raised an alarm, he had the Drotik.

He opened the door of the room. There was a curtain. It was open. He held his ID out in his left hand. Two men stood by the bed where Bagrat Gelashvili lay. Their eyes went to the ID. Arkady extended his right arm and shot the first man in the head, then the second before he could react. The bodies hitting the floor made more sound than the shots.

Gelashvili was awake. His right arm was in a cast, his left handcuffed to the bed. He stared at Korov and opened his mouth to shout. The next shot entered his right eye. It exploded with a soft pop. The wall behind turned red and gray with bits of brain tissue and blood. Korov fired again, into the left eye. Just to make sure.

Orderlies could clean up the blood and mess. They were used to it.

Korov put the PSS away and moved the Drotik to his gun hand, keeping it in his pocket. He stepped out of the room and closed the door. The dead policeman sat in his chair. Korov reentered the main corridor and walked casually to the stairway at the end. That was one of the good things about hospitals. There were plenty of exits. He opened the door and moved quickly down the stairs.

Four dead. Korov checked his watch. Four minutes since he'd killed the guard, more than he'd allotted. He was slipping. Five minutes later, about the time a nurse discovered the dead guard and began screaming, Korov pulled out of the hospital parking lot and disappeared into the traffic of Thessaloniki.

CHAPTER SEVENTEEN

Zviad Gelashvili was at his desk. One of his lieutenants came into the room. The desk was an antique, a glowing masterpiece of 18th Century craftsmanship. Its delicate beauty formed a curious contrast to Zviad's coarse bulk. It was the sort of thing that might have inspired a Japanese Zen master to write a poem.

Behind Zviad two of his bodyguards stood against the wall. They were always present. They were always silent. They were not there to talk.

The man was nervous. Zviad believed in instilling loyalty through rewards. It was profitable to work for Zviad, but there was a second part of the loyalty equation.

Fear.

Zviad had been known to kill the messenger. Looking at his man, he knew something bad had happened.

"Boss..."

"What is it, Iosif?" Zviad had never seen Iosif look nervous. The news must be very bad. He reached for a bottle of vodka and poured two large glasses.

"Drink. Then tell me why you are here."

Iosif gulped down the clear liquor. The words rushed out. "Boss, it's Bagrat. He's dead."

Zviad paused with the glass halfway to his lips. He set it down, carefully. Now he knew why he hadn't heard from his brother. His first thought was disbelief. Bagrat. He was indestructible. His second thought was an odd memory of when they had been children, fighting in the rows of the vineyard. His third thought wasn't a thought. It was feeling that swept over him. Rage.

"How?" His voice was quiet.

"He was in a Greek hospital. Someone shot him. The shooter killed a guard in the hall. Then he went in Bagrat's room and shot a Greek cop and an Interpol agent. Then he shot Bagrat."

"Why was Bagrat in a hospital?"

"A woman put him there. An American. Bagrat tried to grab her. She fought back. Grigor is dead. Bagrat was badly injured, so they took him to the hospital."

"A *WOMAN?*" His shout could be heard throughout the house. Outside the study, his wife listened.

Zviad brought his huge fist down on the antique desk top. It split and sagged. He hit it again. The desk shattered into two parts. The vodka, papers, glasses fell to the floor. The bottle rolled away, gurgling vodka behind it.

Iosif waited, afraid to move.

Zviad shook himself like a great northern bear. He reached down for the vodka, put the bottle to his lips and drank. His mind began planning, calculating. This was now a matter of honor. Bagrat. How had he let this happen?

Once it was known a woman had done this there would be loss of respect. There would be jokes, trouble. An example would have to be made. And who had fired the shots? Who dared?

"Tell me what is known."

Iosif cleared his throat. "Bagrat was under guard. Someone, a man, posed as another Interpol cop. He used a silenced weapon. No one knew anything until a nurse found the guard outside Bagrat's room. No one heard the shots."

"Bagrat and three cops."

"Yes, Boss."

"Go to Greece. Take three men, good ones. Find the woman. Find out anything you can. And Iosif."

"Yes, Boss?"

"I want this woman. And the man who did this. We are clear?"

Iosif was very clear. He was on the chopping block. His only hope was to find the woman or book a one-way ticket to somewhere obscure and far away from Moscow.

"Yes, Boss. Clear."

"Iosif."

"Yes, Boss?"

"Don't come back without her. Go."

Iosif went. He closed the study door behind him. Zviad's wife stepped from the shadows where she'd been listening.

Bedisa had been born and raised in Georgia. She had heard the conversation. She knew honor demanded revenge. She knew Zviad was obsessed with respect. The woman, whoever she was, was as good as dead. She would wish for death many times over if Zviad found her.

She brushed her long black hair back over her shoulders. The movement accented her full breasts. She put her finger to her lips. Iosif watched her. They could hear Zviad pacing back and forth in his study, cursing. His heavy footsteps vibrated out into the hall.

She went to Iosif and ran her fingers over his face, stroked his crotch, kissed him.

"Are you insane?" he hissed. "What if he comes out?"

"He will not come out. I will go in and calm him."

Iosif had been sleeping with Bedisa for the last six months. At first he'd wondered why she'd chosen him, or why he'd let it continue. Perhaps it was the danger. Discovery by Zviad would have been terrible. The fear added an adrenaline rush to their furious and inventive sex.

The sex. Bedisa was not like any other woman he had ever known. She was unique. What she could do with her body, with his, astounded him. She was beautiful, not the kind of woman who normally found Iosif attractive. He knew he was no prize for looks. Iosif was hopelessly in love with her.

After a month she'd begun to talk about Zviad. About Iosif as the new boss. About what they could do together if Zviad was not around any longer.

Zviad was as paranoid as he was shrewd. He had a servant taste his food. He was always protected. He never ventured far from Moscow, though sometimes he went to his villa near Tbilisi, surrounded by bodyguards. He was not an easy man to kill. Bedisa knew Iosif couldn't just kill him and take over. It had to look as if someone else had done it. Otherwise there would be vendettas.

Her voice was soft, almost a whisper. "Find the woman. Then lure Zviad to wherever she is and kill him. We'll never have a better chance."

Iosif nodded. "I don't know..."

Bedisa ran her hand down over his crotch, cupped him and squeezed. She ran her tongue into his ear.

"All right."

"Good."

CHAPTER EIGHTEEN

In Virginia, Harker listened to Nick on her speakerphone.

"No one heard the shots?"

"The first anyone knew was when a nurse found the dead guard. The room was a bloodbath. The Greek cop we were working with was killed. Not much loss there."

"What did the killer look like?"

"Like a cop. He had Interpol ID. The duty nurse had seen one just like it not long before. She thought he was with the others. The receptionist downstairs said he was well-dressed, polite, short hair and cop looking."

"What does that mean?"

"Hard. Cold eyes, like he'd seen too much. Those were her words. The eyes bothered her. He showed her Interpol ID also."

Across the ocean, Nick waited.

"This doesn't feel like a gang hit, someone in competition with the Georgian bunch."

"Silenced weapon, phony ID, clean getaway. More like an agency of some kind. Mossad, CIA, like that."

"If it's an agency, why kill their own agent? "

"Good question. This guy was no ordinary kidnapper. His brother runs the gang. I think he's after Alexander's loot. Someone had to steer him to Greece. Selena thinks we might discover who it was by feeding out information. See what turns up."

"Where would you start?"

"I'm not sure. Gelashvili shouldn't know about us, so why go after Selena? How did he get a photo of her? And who ordered the killings in Greece? Not Gelashvili. There has to be more than one player here."

Sometimes Harker closed her eyes and thought of her father when she needed inspiration. How would he read it? She pictured him sitting in his study in Colorado, sipping bourbon in his green chair. She could almost hear his voice.

She remembered when she'd come home after finishing her second year of college. Worried about choosing the right direction for her future.

"What do you think I should do?"
"What do you want to do?"
"That's not an answer."
The Judge raised his glass and drank, the amber liquid making smoky swirls over the ice. He'd been drinking more lately, since her mother had become ill.
"Yes it is. An answer. You know I can't decide for you. I'd always hoped you'd take up law. But maybe that's not for you."
"It might be. I just don't know"
"What else would you do?"
"I thought medicine."
The Judge laughed. "From the frying pan to the fire. You think law is tough...but you'd be a good doctor. Why medicine?"
"Maybe it sounds naive, but I want to make a difference."
"Law doesn't make a difference?"
"Of course it does."
"Okay," her father had said. "Let's try something. Sometimes I do this when I can't decide what's right. Close your eyes."
She'd closed them.
"Picture yourself as a doctor. Go ahead. Check how it feels in your body, good or bad or neither one."
After a minute she opened her eyes. "It feels like...nothing."
"Okay, keep your eyes closed. Now picture yourself as someone who upholds the law, defends it, practices it."
She'd done it and a wave of heat had passed through her, an inner excitement. She'd opened her eyes.
The Judge had nodded. "See? Now you know what to do."

"Nick."
"Still here, Director."
"Go to Sofia. Our only lead is the inscription in the tomb. I'll clear you into Bulgaria and make it official."
"That means everyone will know who we are."

"Think of it as a way to smoke out whoever's making trouble."

"If I liked bait, I would've taken up fishing."

"You'll handle it. I'll send Ronnie to fish with you."

CHAPTER NINETEEN

Ronnie came in on British Airways via London/Heathrow. He had the look people get when they've just spent too many hours in airports and planes. He hugged Selena. He nodded at Nick. Ronnie didn't shake hands. It wasn't the Navajo custom.

"Never been to Bulgaria before. Anybody start shooting at us yet?"

Nick smiled in spite of himself. "Taxis are over there. We're at the Hilton."

"Kind of high profile."

"We're in the open. Everything's official. The Greeks and the Bulgarians know we're here. For all I know, the Chinese, the Indians and the Pakis. For sure, the Russians. Maybe it will bring someone out of the woodwork. So we might as well enjoy it."

"Works for me."

They got in the cab. "You got a weapon?"

"Yup." he patted his bag.

None of them had been to Bulgaria. Sofia had open air cafes along the boulevard, like every city in Europe. There were ornate apartment buildings, offices and parks. Electric trolley wires ran in ordered webs overhead, like many cities in Europe. Nick couldn't quite put his finger on it, but Sofia was different. Maybe it was the colors on the buildings. Maybe it was the architecture.

They drove past an enormous building.

"Nevsky," the driver pointed. "Very holy."

The cathedral was huge. It had five or six enormous domes that Nick could see. Most of the domes were green with age. Rows of arched windows lined the ground level. It reminded him of a gigantic wedding cake. If he'd had any doubts he wasn't in Western Europe, Nevsky Cathedral removed them.

They met in Ronnie's room. It was a nice room, high up. The hotel was like big city Hiltons everywhere. Except for the room service menu and the hot water on the right, it could have been in St. Louis.

Sofia was set in a broad valley under the shadow of a mountain identified by the tourist guide as Mount Vitosha. From the window of the room they could look out over the city and valley below. The Balkans rose above the valley and formed an ominous wall across the horizon. Snow covered the peaks. Clouds passing in front of the sun threw changing shadows across the slopes. Nick turned away from the hypnotic view.

"Okay. We're here, where the spring and two rivers cross. What now?"

"There used to be a public bath where the springs are. It's a museum now. The only other clue we've got is the reference to Erinys."

"Erinys?" Ronnie went to the mini-fridge, took out a bottle of water, sat on the bed.

"The destructive side of Demeter. Not someone you wanted to meet."

"How do we track it down? You have an idea?"

"It's research, like always. That inscription is from around 146 BCE or so. A lot of Greeks lived in Bulgaria then."

"Not now?"

"Not anymore. The culture is Slavic. Records from that time are lost but there must have been a shrine or temple for Demeter or Erinys. Maybe we can find out where it was. Whoever wrote that inscription would have known about it, assuming it really is a message about the urn."

Nick sat down. "What do you want to do first?"

"Try the libraries and museums, starting with the springs. You and Ronnie can take in the sights."

"Better if we stay together. The bad guys found you in Greece. They could find you here."

"They're not going to go after me in a library or a museum."

"No? Why not?"

"Well, too public?"

"Public doesn't matter. These kind of people don't worry about public."

She knew he was right.

"So we all go to the museum. I hope you're ready to get bored."

"Hey," Ronnie said. "I like museums. Maybe they'll have a Bulgarian dinosaur."

CHAPTER TWENTY

Alexei Ivanovich allowed himself a smile. Korov had displayed his usual efficiency. Zviad Gelashvili was enraged by the death of his brother. Rage and anger were desirable. People who allowed their anger to control them made mistakes.

Alexei had informants inside Zviad's organization. Gelashvili had learned a man had joined the woman, Connor, in Greece. He was convinced it was the same man who had killed Bagrat. Zviad had vowed to skin him alive. He would, if he found him.

Alexei knew Connor's partner was Nicholas Carter, Director of Special Operations for the Project. He knew something about all of the personnel at the Project. He assumed they knew about him. When you reached his level in the world of covert intelligence, many things about you were known. Vysotsky's job as head of Department S meant there were detailed files about him somewhere in Washington. Certainly in the Project.

Intelligence agencies the world over still followed a few unwritten rules. Members of one agency didn't attack their opposite numbers, unless there was a direct and immediate reason to do so. It was a kind of gentlemen's agreement between people who were anything but gentlemen. It provided some security. It wouldn't do to have the various agencies at war with one another, not openly. Deaths brought retaliation. No one wanted a repeat of the bad old days of the cold war.

On the other hand, there was no rule about protecting the competition if someone else went after them. That wasn't his business, unless it was to his advantage. At the moment, Alexei saw no advantage in letting Carter know Gelashvili was stalking him and his partner. Carter was experienced. He would have considered that possibility. It was his lookout.

The two Americans had gone on to Bulgaria and been joined by a third member of their team. They'd registered at a hotel in Sofia. They were making no effort to hide their identity. Alexei found that unusual, even refreshing. It made sense, in an odd way. Carter was well known. Connor was certainly known to Gelashvili. So why hide who they were? He wondered if they were trying to draw Gelashvili into the open. Bulgaria wasn't that far from Moscow. It wasn't like trying to get Zviad to a Western city. It was what he would do in their position. Get him somewhere and talk with him. Forcefully.

Gelashvili might seek his revenge in person. Alexei wanted Korov to be on hand if that happened. He'd ordered Arkady to follow the Americans into Bulgaria. They were the perfect bait to draw Gelashvili away from his Moscow fortress. They could do the work and he could reap the advantages. It was time to eliminate Gelashvili. He would die on foreign soil and no one would suspect Alexei's hand behind events. The more he thought about it, the more he liked it.

If the Americans died as well, it wasn't personal.

CHAPTER TWENTY-ONE

They'd rented a car at the hotel, a Peugeot. They parked in front of the museum.

"More domes." Ronnie gestured at the roof.

The old public baths had a high, arched doorway and paned windows under a large dome. Two more domes at the ends balanced the central mass. The exterior featured horizontal bands of white and brown and accents of yellow under a red roof.

The museum was closed.

"Where to now?" Nick said.

"The National History Museum. It was next on my list."

They'd rented a GPS along with the car. It guided them through the confusion of Sofia traffic and indecipherable street names until they found the National Museum.

The building was modern in a 70s way, low and clean, a study in simplicity. The central foyer was cool and light. The floor was of polished gray stone. A wide flight of stone steps led up to the second and third floors. Exhibition galleries branched off on the sides. Selena consulted a guide printed in English and Bulgarian. The Greek antiquities were on the second floor.

The room with the Greek and Roman exhibits was to the left. White platforms of varying height supported glass cases for the displays. The floor was tiled with more broad squares of polished stone, under a ceiling with repeating squares of dark wood.

The room was quiet and cool. They were the only visitors. Selena walked among the cases looking for anything relating to Erinys or Demeter. The exhibits were arranged chronologically. She moved through the centuries and stopped in front of a case about three feet tall, set at waist height.

"Here's something."

The case contained statues and pottery.

"That's Erinys." She pointed at a damaged statue of a woman in a flowing robe wearing a braided wreath. The sculptor had given her strong, unforgiving features. The corners of her mouth were pulled down. She was looking at something and wasn't happy about it.

Selena read the card below the figure.

"This wasn't found in Sofia. The card says it was dug up in Bankya at a temple dedicated to Demeter."

Nick studied the statue. "Could fit the inscription. Where's Bankya?"

"I don't know."

In the car they consulted the GPS.

"It's about ten kilometers from here." Nick looked at his watch. "Getting late. Let's save it for tomorrow."

They headed back to the Hilton.

CHAPTER TWENTY-TWO

Zviad lay naked on his back, Bedisa on top of his huge belly. Both were slick with sweat. Zviad had his eyes open. He was thinking. Usually after one of their sexual bouts he would fall into a short sleep. Not sleep, really. More like a ten minute escape from reality. A ten minute escape for her.

Not today. Bedisa waited. She knew better than to say anything. Her body rose and fell with Zviad's breathing.

"Iosif called."

She waited.

"The Americans went to Bulgaria, to Sofia. Iosif has gone after them."

"Why Bulgaria?"

"Who knows?" He pushed Bedisa roughly onto the bed and stood.

He pulled on one of the red satin robes he favored. She watched in relief as the robe covered his massive buttocks. It was getting harder to pretend. Zviad's body disgusted her. He smelled. His skin had a greasy quality to it that made her feel dirty. His large penis was about his only redeeming physical quality as far as she was concerned. Iosif wasn't as well endowed, but he could be manipulated in ways impossible with Zviad. If all went well, she wouldn't have to put up with Zviad much longer.

She felt her abdomen where the baby was forming. It would show, soon. Zviad didn't know she was pregnant. Bedisa was sure the child was Iosif's. If Zviad suspected it wasn't his, he would kill her. Before he killed her he would cut her open and rip the child out of her womb. Zviad would know it wasn't his, once the baby was born. He was too clever not to know. It was the reason she had decided to speed up her plans.

"There's talk in town."

"What talk?"

She chose her words carefully. "You know I go to the salons. One of the women I know is married to a man who works for Rokovsky."

Rokovsky was Zviad's principle rival, boss of the Russian gangs in Moscow.

"Fuck Rokovsky. Rokovsky's mother sleeps with diseased beggars who drink slops from the brothels. What talk? Women are always talking."

"She enjoys trying to needle me. She doesn't know I allow it because I learn things useful to you." Zviad was growing impatient. She hurried. This was the dangerous part.

"The Russian thinks you are becoming weak. Bagrat's death has not been avenged. Rokovsky thinks you are afraid to do what has to be done."

Zviad's face grew dark with blood.

"Rokovsky thinks when a man's family is attacked it is a matter of honor. A man who cannot avenge his brother's death is not a man. She was saying you are not honorable. Or a man."

Zviad turned and drove his fist into the wall, smashing through the plaster. "This is what I will do to Rokovsky."

He hit the wall again and turned toward her. For a moment she was afraid. If he hit her like that it would kill her.

"What did you say to her?"

Bedisa smiled.

"I told her I knew that her husband likes men more than women. I wondered what would happen if Rokovsky found out about it. I was very polite. She turned several shades of color, mostly white. I don't think she will be saying these things about you again."

Zviad laughed. "Is it true? About her husband?"

"Yes. I'd heard rumors but I wasn't sure. The way she reacted tells me it's true."

"Good, Bedisa. I own this man now. I will use him."

"There is still the talk, Zviad. Others are wondering. You must move quickly to avenge Bagrat. What will you do?"

Zviad admired himself in a full length mirror.

"I think I will go to Bulgaria. I will make an example of this man. And his woman. An example that will be remembered. Then Rokovsky will understand who he offends. No one will speak of honor then."

Bedisa nodded. It was just what she wanted to hear.

CHAPTER TWENTY-THREE

It was mid-morning the next day. Selena pulled up Bankya on her computer.

"Bankya is an exclusive suburb of Sofia. Lots of ruins, artifacts, mostly pottery and bronze. It has a hotel, hot springs, the old presidential palace. A big tourist draw because of the springs. It's a famous spa and resort. And it has a museum."

"Probably a lot of domes, too," said Ronnie.

Nick had been cleaning his .45. He reassembled it, put it back in the holster and stood. He had a headache.

"Let's get out there and get this over with."

They went down to the lobby, exited the hotel and got in the Peugeot. Arkady Korov watched them leave. He got in his rental and pulled out a safe distance behind. Just another battered gray Renault, one of many. They'd never see him. He followed them out of town. Signs pointed the way to Bankya.

Why Bankya, Arkady wondered. Maybe they were going for the waters.

Earlier he'd spoken with Alexei Ivanovich.

"Gelashvili believes the Americans killed his brother. He's gone after them. He should have arrived in Sofia by now. Sooner or later he will be where they are. Your primary mission is his elimination. The Americans may accomplish that for you."

"Understood."

"Arkady. In this instance, the Americans are a means to an end. Observe them and learn what you can. Do not see them as your enemy."

Korov had said nothing. Orders were orders.

CHAPTER TWENTY-FOUR

Sofia and Mount Vitosha were prominent in the view from the outskirts of Bankya as they drove in. The found the only museum.

"Maybe they'll have a dinosaur." Ronnie sounded hopeful.

There were no dinosaurs. In the museum they learned that the temple of Demeter was buried under a church outside the town. They left the museum and stood in the sunshine.

"What now?"

"Lunch, Ronnie. Then we'll check out the church."

They found a cafe. A dozen tables were set behind a low wooden fence and gate. Trees branched overhead. It was a pleasant spot.

"It's nice out." Selena took a deep breath of fresh spring air. "We can sit outside."

They ordered a spicy beef stew, bread and coffee. A large salad of tomatoes, cucumbers, onions, roasted peppers and an unfamiliar cheese. The food was good.

Korov watched them from a bench under a tree. His car was parked nearby. He held a local paper in front of him and pretended to read. He wore workman's clothes and a cloth cap. From time to time the Americans scanned the area. Their eyes lingered on him for a moment and passed on. Arkady knew it was automatic. They hadn't made him. The woman seemed absorbed in her food.

Then he saw one of Gelashvili's men. He was talking on his cell phone.

Five minutes later two cars drove by. Zviad Gelashvili was in the second one. The man with the phone got into the first car. Korov counted five men plus Gelashvili. In the cafe, the Americans had finished their meal. They stood up to leave. They got in their car and drove off. Gelashvili and his men followed.

Korov stood and folded his paper. The others were still in sight. He got in the car, started it up and pulled out after them.

What was the American expression?

Showtime.

CHAPTER TWENTY-FIVE

The Church of St. George was some distance outside of town, on a side road off the main highway. It was made of whitewashed stone and shaped like a cross. Wooden scaffolding rose along one side, a pile of debris littered beneath it. The church had a high arched entryway and a neglected look. A central bell tower rose to a single green dome topped by an Orthodox cross. The hillside above the church was dotted with old buildings sliding into disrepair. A monastery, from the looks of it long abandoned. Not much was happening at the church of St. George.

The entrance doors were made of heavy wooden planks and locked with a large, rusted padlock that looked like it might have been new when the church was built.

Nick looked around.

"No sign of a caretaker. We need to get inside." He jiggled the lock. It was old but it was strong.

Ronnie walked over to the junk under the scaffolding. He poked around in the debris, stooped and picked up a two foot length of steel rebar.

"Try this."

"You're going to break in?" Selena said.

"You got a better idea?"

Nick inserted the rebar through the u-shape of the lock, braced against the door and levered down. The lock broke. He tossed it aside. He pulled one of the doors open. They stepped inside and he pulled the door closed behind them.

The interior was lit by sunlight filtering through an arched stained glass window picturing St. George slaying the dragon. In the front of the church, the altar was draped in a red cloth and backed by three large wooden screens. Exposed beams blackened with age crossed the ceiling high above the church floor. Lamps of cut glass hung on long chains at regular intervals. Doors to either side of the altar led to the arms of the cross. The faint aftermath of incense lingered over rows of carved wooden pews.

Next to the door was a dusty wooden table with brochures. Selena picked one up.

"The current building dates from 1664," she read. "The original church was built in the eleventh century on the ruins of a Greek temple dedicated to the goddess of the harvest."

"Demeter," Nick said.

"This mentions the statue of Erinys. It was found during the reconstruction. The brochure says the temple site still exists under the present building."

She kept reading. "The Greek temple was located over a natural limestone formation of caves that are thought to have been an ancient mineral spring. When the first church was built the caves were converted into crypts for the monks."

"You mean they're still there?" Nick picked up a brochure.

"Looks like it. They stopped putting bodies in after the new church was built."

"If it was part of the Greek temple there might be something there."

"Sure there is," Ronnie said. "Lots of bones. Dead monks."

"Hell, we've come this far. This is our last shot. After this we have no leads."

"I don't like bones." Ronnie shook his head.

"You wanted to see a dinosaur."

"That's different. Those are big bones. Lizard kind of bones. Human bones, they're bad luck."

"Boys." Selena interrupted. "Cut it out. Let's look for an entrance."

There was nothing obvious. They looked in the rooms to the side of the church. After twenty minutes they still hadn't found it.

Selena looked down at an old Turkish rug placed to the side of the altar.

"Nice rug. Probably two hundred years old." She looked around. The rest of the floor behind the altar was unadorned.

"Why put a rug here?" she said. She lifted the corner and pulled it aside. A wooden door was set into the floor with a ring at either end. Ronnie and Nick lifted it away. A flight of narrow steps descended into blackness. A dry, old smell drifted up to meet them.

"Déjà vu all over again," Nick said.

"It's not the same. We know what's down there this time." Even so, Selena seemed nervous. The last time the three of them had gone down a flight of steps into the dark it had almost killed them.

"We need light."

"You don't have your flashlight? I thought you always carried one."

She was right. He usually did.

"Not this time." Nick went to the altar. He took down two large candles. "These will do." There were matches. He lit the candles, handed one to Ronnie and walked over to the opening.

The steps ended twenty feet below. A narrow passage led away into darkness between rough stone walls. They started down the steps.

CHAPTER TWENTY-SIX

Sometimes Elizabeth wished she'd decided to become a doctor after all. Maybe an obstetrician. That would be good, to bring new life into the world. Or a surgeon. High tech lasers. Powerful glasses, blue scrubs and masks. The quiet sounds of technology in the background while her dedicated team helped her cut out bad things that made people ill and crazy.

The files that crossed her desk on any given day would make people crazy. Send them screaming into the streets if they knew what was in them. A terrorist plot aimed at killing fifty thousand people, barely stopped in time. A nuclear device gone missing. The latest from North Korea. A memo about possible gas attacks in the New York Subway.

Elizabeth often found a pattern where others saw unrelated pieces. Right now she didn't like what she was thinking. Her intuition was ringing alarms. The Pentagon's connection to CDC, Weinstein and Campbell bothered her. They were hiding something. That was nothing new, but what were they hiding?

Sophisticated bombs had killed two scientists, brutal murder a third. All three were tied together by the urn and what might or might not be in it, the key to a devastating crop disease.

She sipped water and swallowed two aspirins. She took a yellow pad from her drawer and uncapped FDR's pen. Sometimes she liked to write things down. To sort out her thoughts. It was slower, more intimate than the computer. It helped her think. She made a list.

C,M,W killed, two bombs. Semtex. Who?
Pentagon?
Myth/Demeter/Persephone/Urn
Crop blight
Attack/Selena/Leak Who?
Hospital shootings/Greece

There were too many things on that list. What was the Pentagon connection? There might be a way to find out. She triggered her intercom.

"Steph, could you come in for a minute?"

"Right there, Director."

Stephanie came into the office and sat. When it came to hacking into high security systems, Steph had no equal.

"What's up?"

"I have a tricky job for you. The Pentagon."

"You want me to hack in?"

"Yes."

"DIA?"

"Depends on what you find. There are a couple of things I'm looking for."

Steph waited.

"First we need to know what they're doing with CDC. Why was Campbell upset?"

"Okay."

"Find out if they have a bio-warfare plan involving crops or crop blight. Anything you can. They mustn't know it was us."

"What's second?"

"If you come across something, see if you can find out who authorized it."

"It will take a day or two. They'll never notice."

"Good enough. I'd like you to do it right away."

Steph got up and headed for her computers. Elizabeth picked up her pen and began tapping. She felt her chest tighten, her breath getting short. Time for her shot, she'd forgotten. She set the pen down. She opened her drawer, took out a hypodermic and a glass vial, measured out the dose and injected her thigh. In a minute she felt better. Her disease was halted, under control. But she had to pay attention.

Her lungs would never recover. She wouldn't be running any marathons, but at least she was alive. She wished there was someone who could be with her, if it ever got worse. But there wasn't anyone.

She'd been single since a relationship gone wrong when she was a lot younger. She didn't have much time for relationships. She had a Brownstone in Georgetown, the ear of the President, a new Audi and more real power than most of the men who ran things in the nation's Capitol. But she didn't have anyone to share it with when she went home. She'd accepted there might not ever be someone. Her work had become her lover.

She took two more aspirin and looked at the list again.

Someone had leaked the information on the tablets. It was only a question of time until she knew who. Then she might find out who had killed Campbell and the others and sent thugs after Selena. The only thing certain was that it all centered around the urn.

Elizabeth leaned back in her chair. One step at a time.

CHAPTER TWENTY-SEVEN

The passage at the foot of the stairs went straight for about twenty feet and made a right angle turn to the left. It opened into a long, high cave, hollowed out by the old mineral springs. The cave was dark. It had irregular walls with strange shapes hanging from the ceiling. Nick felt like it was ready to swallow him.

The bones started right away.

He didn't know what he'd expected. Maybe skeletons, wrapped in moldering rags. Maybe dried out, leathery bodies. Coffins. It wasn't like that.

Arched, oven-shaped shelves lined the walls. The shelves were piled with bones. Some shelves were filled with thigh bones stacked like firewood. Some with arm bones, others with the small bones of feet and hands. Some were filled with rows of empty skulls staring at nothing. Hundreds of skulls had been fastened onto the walls. They climbed and curved over the shelves. The light from the candles flickered and danced over the bones.

The bones were mute. The skulls had nothing to say. The crypt smelled of dust and centuries of silence.

"Guess the monks liked the idea of community," Nick said.

Ronnie held his candle high and peered at the skulls. "Gives me the creeps."

They walked toward the far end of the chamber. A thousand empty eyes followed them.

All that was left of the temple of Demeter was a cracked wall of marble and slabs underfoot. A large block of stone stood in the center of the slabs. It bore dark and ancient stains. A large niche had been cut into the wall. It was empty.

"Why down here?" Ronnie said. "Wouldn't they put it up on the surface?"

"Demeter and Persephone were worshiped in something called the Eleusinian Mysteries," Selena said. "The main temple was probably up top. Down here would be for secret rites by the priests. It's a cave, it's perfect. That big stone is an altar, probably for animal sacrifices. Ronnie, give me your candle."

She took it from him and held it up. On the wall over the niche was the figure of a horse.

"There's Persephone's symbol again. Looks like a dead end."

"We're in the right place for it," Ronnie said.

Nick heard a scrape of something on stone. His ear began to burn.

"Douse the light." His voice was quiet. "Someone's coming."

They blew out the candles. The chamber went black. At least there aren't any spiders. He drew his .45. Maybe it was a priest, wondering why the crypt was open. Maybe not.

A gleam of light showed at the entrance to the cave. Someone with a flashlight. Then a second beam. A large man stepped into the cave, silhouetted by the light behind. He held a flashlight in one hand, a gun in the other.

Not a priest. Not smart, either.

A second man followed. He had a gun. Another light moved behind him.

At least three. Maybe more behind or upstairs.

The first man flicked his light over the piles of bones. The probing beam found Selena against the old temple wall, her Glock extended in both hands. He shouted and raised his gun.

Nick shot the first man and dove for cover behind the stone altar. A second later Ronnie followed. Selena dropped to the floor. Everyone began firing. Muzzle blasts lit the crypt at both ends, painting the skulls and bones in brief flashes. The noise of the guns filled the cave. Fragments of ancient bone spiraled into the air. He felt the wind of passing bullets. Rounds ricocheted from the walls and the altar and whined around the cave in the dark. The second shooter went down. Then the third.

Silence. Nick's ears were ringing. No one else came out of the passage.

"Anyone hit?"

"No." Selena's voice was tight. "This damn floor is hard."

"Me neither." Ronnie's voice was soft.

"I'm moving right." Nick shuffled to the right, came to Selena climbing to her feet.

"Stay behind me. Don't get too close."

He felt his way along the wall. His hand touched bone, teeth, the rough edge where an eye had been. He jerked his hand back and kept moving. He reached the passage.

Selena and Ronnie came up behind.

Three bodies lay by the entrance to the passage. They weren't moving. Blood pooled around them. A lot of blood. Their bowels had let go. The stench made Nick choke.

Selena stepped over them without thinking. She'd taken four steps before she realized what she'd just done. Three dead men. She might as well have stepped over bags of trash, for all the feeling she had about it. The realization rocked her.

"What do you think, Ronnie?" Nick's voice was quiet.

"Might be more around the corner. Bound to be more upstairs."

"It's like Fallujah. Remember that factory?"

"Yeah, I remember."

Nick crouched down and took a fast look around the corner.

"It's clear to the steps."

The steps were only wide enough for one person at a time. Anyone up top would have a clean shot at them as they came out.

"Fallujah, we had grenades. This sucks, Kemo Sabe."

"Kemo Sabe? You going native on me?"

"I always wanted to say that. Tonto always said that to the Lone Ranger when the shit was about to hit the fan. Kemo Sabe. Has a nice ring to it."

"What does it mean?"

"You don't want to know."

Selena said, "If you're done..." They turned to her. "How do we get out of here?"

"The altar's not far away, ahead and to the right. We go up one at a time and get behind it." Nick grinned at her. "Fast."

He ran up the stairs and came out of the opening and rolled forward behind the altar. The sound of an Uzi on full auto echoed in the church above. The screens behind the altar shattered. Shards of old wood bounced down the steps. They heard Nick's .45 lay down covering fire.

"You last. We'll cover you."

Ronnie went up the stairs like Nick had done and disappeared. In a second Selena heard his Glock. Overhead it sounded like World War III. She pictured the altar, the space behind it. She took a deep breath. The adrenaline kicked in and she ran up the stairs.

CHAPTER TWENTY-EIGHT

Alexei Ivanovich tapped his fingers on his desk . His day had just become far more difficult. He looked at the flash drive in his hand and thought about what it contained. He read the note again. It was printed in English.

Do not jump to conclusions. In this matter, the Project is with you.
It was signed.
A friend.

The package and note had arrived by UPS that morning. Alexei had gotten many odd communications over the years. Sometimes in a dark street at night. Sometimes by official notice. Sometimes in a hard room where unbearable pain was the prelude to truth.

Never by way of UPS. He knew the trail would lead nowhere if he traced it. The video featured the Director of the American CIA talking about a plot against Russia, code named Demeter.

Do not jump to conclusions.

Alexei translated the meaning. Don't make a quick judgment without knowing the facts. Therefore, don't take uninformed action. It was an American idiom. It was logical to assume an American had sent it. Why would an American send such a damaging video to him?

In this matter, the Project is with you.

The sender must be someone in the American intelligence agencies. No one else would know about the Project or how to get the video to Alexei.

Alexei knew he should go to his boss. If he did, all hell would break loose. The Kremlin was paranoid enough without this.

Do not jump to conclusions.

Someone wanted him to know the Director of American Central Intelligence plotted against Russia. Someone wanted him stopped and wanted Alexei's help. Someone wanted him to see the Project as an ally.

Only one explanation made sense. It wasn't a sanctioned operation. That made it a danger to both nations. Alexi considered the possibility the video was part of a larger scheme with a hidden end in mind, suspect as three day old fish in the market. If it wasn't faked it was the kind of thing that could lead to war. Alexei didn't think it was faked.

Vysotsky sometimes felt he lived in a world of brittle mirrors, a world of infinite reflections and possible realities, one within the other to infinity. Truth was out there, but it was often unpleasant and hard to find.

Do not jump to conclusions.

The Project was small. SVR was massive. The Project had no ability to mount any significant operation within Russia. SVR had all the resources it needed to do exactly that. The situation was reversed in America. The Project could operate there in ways Alexei could not. The bow was drawn in America, but the arrow was aimed at Russia. Whoever had sent the video wanted an alliance of convenience against a common enemy.

Alexei made a decision. He picked up his satellite phone and called Korov.

CHAPTER TWENTY-NINE

Korov followed Gelashvili and the Americans to the church of St. George. The church was well back from the paved road, isolated on the side of a hill. It was reached by a long gravel drive in poor repair. Abandoned buildings dotted the slope above it. He parked a hundred feet away and considered his next move.

His phone vibrated. Only General Vysotsky had that number.

"Yes."

"Things have changed. What is your situation?"

"Gelashvili has followed the Americans. They are all in a church outside Bankya. He will try to kill them."

"You will prevent that. Kill Gelashvili. Protect the Americans. Do not reveal yourself."

"Protect the Americans?"

"At all costs. Repeat your orders."

"Kill Gelashvili. Protect the Americans."

Gunshots echoed inside the church.

"Sir. Shooting in the church."

"You have your orders."

The connection terminated.

Arkady put the phone back in his pocket and drew the Drotik from his shoulder holster. He ran to the church, pulled open the door and slipped inside.

In the rainbow light coming through the stained glass window, Korov saw Gelashvili and two of his men halfway down the main aisle. They crouched behind pews, firing in bursts toward the front of the church. Two pistols answered from behind the altar. As he watched, a woman come up out of the floor and rolled forward behind the altar, firing three shots as she went.

One of Gelashvili's men crawled to a side aisle and moved toward the front. A large, life-like painted statue of Mary decked in a blue robe and golden crown shielded him from the altar. In a moment he would have an angle on the Americans.

The Drotik was an accurate pistol. The 5.6 mm rounds were high velocity, flat trajectory. Korov was an excellent marksman. It was an easy shot. He raised the pistol, flicked the selector to full and touched the trigger. The sound ripped through the air like tearing cloth. Zviad's man cried out and sprawled lifeless on the church floor.

Behind the altar, Nick turned to Ronnie.

"What the hell was that?"

"Don't know. Not an Uzi."

"Shit."

More shots. The ripping sound again, a cry of mortal pain. Nick looked out from behind the altar. A large, bearish man rose between the pews. He screamed in rage, firing at someone in the back of the church. The ripping sound came again, accompanied by a brilliant second or two of muzzle flash. The bearish man looked down and put a hand on his chest. He swayed. He fell forward, crashing into the pews.

Someone ran to the entrance and disappeared outside.

"Hey!" Nick yelled after him. He heard a car start, tires spinning on gravel, an engine fading into the distance.

The church was silent as the crypt below. They stood and walked down among the pews. Ronnie pointed at a body spread eagled on the floor.

"That one over there. Would have had a clear shot if someone hadn't interfered."

"Yeah. A good Samaritan. With a high end auto pistol."

"Not American or European."

"Something we haven't heard before."

Selena still had the Glock in her hand. She looked down at the dead men. "Who are they?"

"I don't know. Looking at the clothes, I'd say it might be the same bunch that tried to grab you in Greece."

He pushed at Gelashvili's dead bulk with his shoe. "Lousy cut. Someone ought to clue these people in about their tailor."

CHAPTER THIRTY

"Did you have to shoot up a church?" Harker sounded annoyed.

Nick held the phone in his left hand. His right wrapped around a whiskey. Sofia at night filled the view from the window. The lights were on, the city a fairytale picture of domes and old buildings. The dark shape of the Balkans loomed against a night sky filled with glittering stars. It was like something from a Walt Disney movie. The only things missing were Pinocchio and Jiminy Cricket.

"No choice. They picked the spot. They called the game. They lost. Simple as that."

Nick contemplated the lights of the city. He was coming down from the fight in the church. He felt edgy, wired. His hand gripped the whiskey. How many more times was he going to do this before his luck ran out?

"The men you shot were from the same gang that tried to take Selena in Greece. One of them was Zviad Gelashvili. You took out one of the biggest Russian crime bosses in the world."

"It wasn't us who killed him."

"What do you mean?"

"Someone else is in the game. One man."

"Why didn't you say so before?"

"Hadn't gotten to it. Now I have."

"Who?"

"I don't know. He used a specialized pistol. Full auto, very high rate of fire. Small rounds. Can't be many of those."

"That sounds military."

"Has to be."

"Gelashvili was based in Moscow. Maybe it was Russian."

"Why would the Russians help us out?"

"Maybe they didn't. Maybe they just wanted Gelashvili. He was a problem for them."

"They know who we are. Helping us doesn't make sense."

Nick heard her sigh over the phone. "What about that urn?"

"What about it? There's nothing to tell us what happened to it. No leads at all."

"You're sure?"

"Unless Selena can turn something up. There wasn't anything under that church."

"All right. If you can't get any new intel, come home."

"Roger that." Nick put down the phone.

Selena came out of the bathroom, wrapped in a white robe. Her hair was unkempt, damp. She'd had several drinks before she went into the bathroom. She had a whiskey in her hand. She drained it and poured another from the bottle. It was her fifth, or maybe her sixth. Nick had never seen her drink that much, especially whiskey. Selena was a wine drinker. Hard liquor wasn't her thing.

"How you feeling?"

"Fine." She sat on the couch, drank. He sat down next to her. She smelled of soap and lemon shampoo and some fresh scent that was her. Her breath was strong with whiskey. Maybe she'd had another during her bath.

"Good whiskey," she said. "Helps, at the end of a busy day."

She was beginning to slur her words. He said nothing.

"Another busy day." She raised her glass at him. It wavered. "Get up, see the sights, have lunch. Shoot a few people. Back to the hotel in time for dinner."

"Selena..."

She drank. Her glass was empty. She got off the couch, staggered a little as she went to the bottle and poured another drink.

"Maybe you've had enough."

She rounded on him. Liquid slopped from her glass. "Don't you tell me I've had enough. I'll know when I've had enough."

"What's the matter?"

"What's the matter? What the hell do you think 'sa matter? You made me into a fucking killer."

That's not fair. He didn't say it.

"Oh, shit." She set the glass down, dropped down on the sofa. "Din't mean that."

"I know." He put his arm around her. She put her head on his shoulder.

"Jus' stepped over 'em. Like they were garbage."

It took a second for him to figure out what she meant.

"They were garbage. Those were bad people."

"But they were people. We killed 'em."

"They would have killed us."

"Darwin."

"What?"

"Darwin. Su'vival of the fisstest. Fittest."

Her face turned white. She clapped a hand over her mouth, jumped up and ran for the bathroom. He heard her vomit into the toilet.

Nick waited. The sounds of retching stopped. He heard water running. In a few moments she came to the door.

"Come on, bed time." He helped her into the bedroom and out of her robe. She crawled under the covers.

"Sorry," she mumbled. Then she was out.

Nick went back into the living area and turned out the lights. Sofia sparkled in chains of light along the valley floor. For no reason at all he thought of the closing scene in Gone With The Wind.

Tomorrow was another day.

He used the bathroom, brushed his teeth, went into the bedroom, undressed. He got into bed. Selena snored.

He stared at the ceiling, thinking. She'd been drunk, but the words stung, even though he knew they were untrue. She'd chosen her new life. Not him. He thought of Megan.

What he'd felt for Megan and what he felt for Selena were two different things. Love was too simple a word. The word itself confused him. Megan had been so different.

Megan had been at ease with herself and with him. She'd lived in a world far removed from the desolate places where death shaped his days and nights. If she hadn't died, Megan's world could have been his world. He would have left the Corps, become a normal civilian. Never made his appointment with a child and a grenade in Afghanistan. Never met Harker or Selena.

Megan's world had been peaceful. No one would call the world he shared with Selena peaceful. The strain was beginning to show. Selena was becoming more volatile. She wasn't sleeping well. Sometimes he'd see her gazing off at nothing in particular. She was getting the look. He knew she was headed for a moment of truth. Sooner or later, everyone who made violent death part of their job came to that moment. He didn't know how she'd handle it. Maybe he'd talk with Harker about it.

He closed his eyes. It was a long time before he slept. He dreamed.

He's back in the dust of the Afghan street, again. He's in the market, like always. The AKs begin, like they always do. He ducks into a doorway, as he always does. The child runs toward him with the grenade, again. He raises his rifle.

This time, the dream is different. This time, someone is standing off to the side. It's a woman. A naked woman, dark, as if she were standing in deep shade. She looks at him. Her eyes aren't human, they're like deep pools of black with stars in them. The child throws the grenade. He feels the rifle kick back against his shoulder and the child's face changes into Selena's. Everything goes white.

Nick sat up in bed, gasping. Sweat covered him. The sheet under him was soaked. Next to him, Selena had fallen into a deep sleep.

The dream had changed. It had never changed before. It was always the same, playing out the day in Afghanistan when he almost died. It had twisted his nights for years. For a while, it had come less often. Now it was back. Now it had changed.

Who was the woman? No woman stood naked in that Afghan village three years ago. Something had been different about the child's face. Then he remembered. It shook him.

He got up and waited for tomorrow.

CHAPTER THIRTY-ONE

Selena had been quiet on the long trip home from Bulgaria. Nick doubted she remembered much about what she'd said in the hotel. He hadn't brought it up with her. He'd decided not to talk with Harker. Selena was part of his team and it was his job to watch out for her. Harker had enough on her plate.

The night before he'd dreamed of Afghanistan again. The dark woman wasn't in it. The child's face stayed the same, an Afghan child. He'd been up since 3:00 A.M. Drinking coffee and staring out the window. Thinking about Selena.

She didn't know him, not really. He tried to remember how it had been when Megan was alive. Had she known him? It was a question he'd never asked himself. He'd been different, he knew that. When she died he'd shut something down. Sometimes it felt like he had a steel wall around him that kept everyone out. Selena had breached it.

When Harker offered him a civilian job he'd thought he was done shooting at people. He'd lead a normal life. A quiet life. Got that one wrong, he thought. He had no idea what a normal life was anymore. One day at a time.

Nick looked around the room. Everyone was together in Harker's office for the first time in weeks. Even Lamont was back. His mom had named him after Lamont Cranston, the Shadow of radio fame. In the Seals they'd called him Shadow. The nickname had stuck.

Lamont had Ethiopian ancestors. It showed up in his wiry body, all muscles and tendons that stood out like ropes. He had blue eyes and coffee shaded skin. A hard ridge of white and pink scar tissue ran from his forehead across the bridge of his nose down onto his cheek, a souvenir of Iraq. He wore a blue sling and soft cast on his injured arm. It was a big improvement over the rigid plaster he'd sported since Khartoum.

Harker held up a flash drive. It was black and shiny.

"This came yesterday. By UPS, if you can believe it. No explanation, no note."

She was wired. Nick couldn't remember the last time he'd seen her look like that. She kept tapping her damn pen. He wished she would stop. Maybe it was that last drink from the night before, but his headache wouldn't quit.

Harker inserted the drive in a slot on her desk. The big monitor on the wall lit up and showed a windowless room. The walls were featureless. Five men sat at a smooth wooden table. Two had their backs to the camera. The lighting and quality of the video were good, but the field was narrow. Nick figured it had been taken by a concealed camera, maybe in the wall.

One of the men facing the camera was in his 60s, elegant, immaculate in a dark suit that signaled money and power. His shirt gleamed with the look only a five hundred dollar tailored shirt can achieve. He wore a tie that had probably come from the same place as the shirt. His hair was silver, perfect, sculpted by an artist.

Wendell Lodge, Director of Central Intelligence.

From the back, one of the men they couldn't see seemed vaguely familiar, but Nick couldn't place it. The other wore civilian clothes and a close haircut. He had a military feel about him. Something in the way he sat. Lodge was talking. The audio was unintelligible.

Harker said, "The audio clears up in a moment. The man to Lodge's left is Harold Dansinger. You all know who Dansinger is?"

Everyone did. A rich man who'd made his fortune in agriculture, Dansinger was a major force behind genetically altered foods. Grains were his mainstay. Wheat. Rice. Corn. Barley. Millet. The bread grains and basic foods of most of the world.

Carter had seen ads for Dansinger's products. They showed him smiling under a trademark white Stetson, his hand stretched out toward golden fields of corn rolling in green rows to the horizon. A few happy bluebirds glided in a cheerful sunlit sky. Homey letters spelled out *"Hal Dansinger, The Farmer's Friend."* Below that the ads read *"Dansinger Enterprises: Putting American Food on the Tables of the World."*

Nick pictured the ad in his mind. He thought Dansinger looked like a used car salesman who'd just sold another clunker for a nice profit.

"I wouldn't touch his food with a pole," Selena said. "He engineers his products to destroy natural competition. Once you plant Dansinger's rice or corn, that's all you can grow."

"What's Lodge talking about?" Ronnie asked.

"Wait."

The audio cleared in mid sentence.

"--April. Long range weather forecast is favorable over the Ukraine and Western Russia. Demeter is ready."

"You are sure everything is in place?" Dansinger's voice was dry and without warmth. He was in his late sixties, large boned and raw, weathered from years under the Texas sun.

Lodge answered Dansinger's question. "Yes." He paused. "Before we go on, I'd like to make sure we are all in agreement."

One of the men at the table stood. "I am not. Wendell, I agree with our goal, but not this. The suffering will be immense if we implement. It's conceivable millions could die. I can't be a party to this."

Harker gestured. "That's George Wilkinson, head of BRES."

BRES was Biological Research Engineering Solutions, the world's leading authority on boosting third world agricultural economies. If there were crop problems in Southeast Asia or Africa, you called BRES. Wilkinson was a genius. He was also recently dead.

Carter's ear began itching.

"I understand your hesitation, George. I feel the same way. There's no decision to implement as yet. But Demeter is ready if the Russians push us too far." He gestured at the short haired man with his back toward them, who nodded.

"This is simply preparation. We'll be sorry to lose you. Of course I trust in your discretion about our discussions."

"I signed the paper, Wendell, I'm not going to say anything. But this is wrong. I think you must reconsider." He looked at his watch. "I have to get back to Washington. Gentlemen."

Wilkinson left the room. There was a brief silence. Dansinger spoke.

"He's a problem, Wendell."

Lodge glanced down at notes on the table. "No, Harold, he's not."

"Then I can report to the others that he will not interfere?"

"You may."

The screen blanked.

"Do you think it's legitimate?" Nick asked Harker.

"I do. We can analyze it, but I don't think it's faked."

"Wilkinson's dead."

"The implication is clear. Lodge had Wilkinson killed because he wouldn't go along with the plan, whatever it is."

"But why? That's over the top, even for Langley."

"If Lodge had Wilkinson killed, it's not official. He's gone rogue. He's planning something unauthorized about Russia. I'm going to have to go to the President. Damn."

"Who could have sent this, Director?"

"Good question, Nick. Someone who doesn't like Lodge. Someone who can't come out in the open."

"At Langley?"

"Maybe."

She set the pen down. Everyone watched her.

"This is all we needed," she said. "Up against the CIA."

"We're not up against CIA," Nick said. "We're up against Lodge. I get along with Hood and Hood wants to be DCI. Maybe I could approach him. See if he's got any knowledge of what Lodge is doing."

Clarence Hood was DNCS at Langley, Director of National Clandestine Services. In charge of field operations everywhere in the world.

"We can't risk that. What if he's part of it?" Elizabeth picked up her pen again. "I'm going to get a new autopsy on Wilkinson. We will now assume Lodge has gone rogue. We need to be careful. Whoever sent this expects us to do something about it. They may be trying to set us up for their own ends."

She looked at them. "Maybe I don't have to say this, but everyone needs to watch it."

"So," Ronnie said, "what else is new?"

CHAPTER THIRTY-TWO

Harker had been to the White House many times, but it never failed to impress her. She waited in an anteroom outside the Oval Office. Two Secret Service agents stood nearby. The dark suits and earpieces they wore were as much a part of the White House culture as the flag flying over the building.

The building carried a tangible aura of power. Everyone who came here felt it. Everyone serious about politics wanted to be here. The White House was more than a pretty building or a symbol. It was the beating heart of the most powerful nation on earth. The man in the next room was the most important politician in the world.

There had been good presidents and bad ones. There were a few great ones. Elizabeth thought James Rice was one of the great ones. Like all powerful leaders, he was surrounded by people who tried to please and mislead him. They tended to tell him what he wanted to hear and conceal their agendas. That was especially true of the intelligence community, the big agencies.

Rice had created the Project to make sure he knew the things no one else would tell him. The Project alerted him to problems before they became more serious threats. More, it gave him a way to eliminate those problems without the interference of self-serving politicians. Elizabeth's unit operated under a budget blacker than the far side of Pluto.

What she was going to tell him was political dynamite. Worse. DCI Lodge had helped clean up a conspiracy that would have torn the country apart. It was Harker's team that had broken it up. They'd left a mess and questions that couldn't be asked in public. Lodge had been Acting Director at that time and he'd been useful. The Director's spot at Langley was his reward. Rice had to do what was best for the country, even if he didn't trust Lodge or like him. The President wasn't going to enjoy what she told him today.

An aide stepped through a curved door in the wall.

"You can go in, Director. He's ready for you."

"Thank you." She stood and smoothed the black linen pants suit she'd chosen for this meeting.

Rice rose from behind Teddy Roosevelt's desk and came out to greet her.

"Elizabeth. Thanks for coming."

That was Rice's style. She'd requested the meeting but he was making her feel as if she were doing him a favor. The Secret Service agent standing by the wall displayed no expression.

Rice was just short of six feet tall. He wore a dark blue suit and red tie. He still had a muscular look that hinted at when he'd been a young Marine officer in Vietnam. He wasn't particularly handsome, but it didn't matter. You got the feeling in his presence that you were the most important thing in his life at that exact moment. He had charisma, in spades. He was also a very intelligent man.

"Thank you for seeing me on such short notice, Mr. President."

"I can give you ten minutes, Director." He walked over to the couch and gestured. They sat down.

"It's not good news, is it?"

"No sir. We have a situation. It might be best if we were alone."

"That bad?" Rice turned to the agent. "Eddie, please wait outside."

"Sir...?

"I know, you're supposed to stay. Wait outside. Director Harker is not going to attack me."

"Yes, Mr. President."

The door closed behind him.

Elizabeth had reviewed the autopsy on Wilkinson. At her insistence, the coroner had taken a second look. That had turned up a tiny puncture mark and faint signs consistent with being held down on a soft surface. No one would have noticed unless they were looking. Someone had shot him up with air. When the bubble reached his heart it hit him like a bomb. Wilkinson had been murdered.

She gave Rice a no frills summation of what she'd learned, the video, Wilkinson, the talk of Russia. Campbell's comments about the Pentagon. Her certainty that the deaths of the three research scientists were related.

"You believe this video is genuine."

"Yes, sir. I am certain it is."

"Director, you are telling me the Director of the CIA is a traitor, or at best a murderer."

"Yes, sir, that is my conclusion."

"You can't prove it."

"No, sir. Not so a court would convict him."

Rice stood. She rose with him. He walked over to the windows facing out on the Rose Garden.

"Things are touchy with Russia right now. I'm trying to keep things calm about our missiles in Eastern Europe. The opposition is gearing up for the nomination and waiting for me to show any sign of weakness. If Lodge is promoting some cowboy adventure..."

He left the thought unfinished. He turned back to face her.

"What is your advice?"

"Sir, we can't go after him yet. I've alerted my team. I'm seeking more intel. It's all I can do until there's something more specific."

"I can't just remove him," Rice said. "He knows where all the bodies are buried. The son of a bitch is worse than Hoover ever was and it's an election year. He'd find a way to make trouble. Do you think you can handle this for me?"

Elizabeth thought there were many levels to that statement, but she didn't say so.

"I'll do my best, sir. It's what you pay me for."

"Very well." Rice went to the desk, pressed a button. A door opened. An aide entered. She started from the room.

"Director."

"Sir?"

"Thank you."

"You're welcome, Mr. President."

Welcome to another crisis in the works, she thought. She was glad she wasn't the one sitting in that office.

CHAPTER THIRTY-THREE

Elizabeth studied an elegant card engraved with the crest of the Russian embassy.

Dimitri Yakov
Second Cultural Attaché

The card had arrived that morning. A note was written on the back in black ink.

Washington Monument. 14:30 today.

Yakov was SVR's chief resident in Washington. He wanted a meeting. It didn't surprise her that SVR knew who she was. What surprised her was that they wanted to talk. Communication between US intelligence agencies and SVR was non-existent. Yakov knew she wouldn't refuse.

Yakov had been seconded from Department S. He would never arrange a meeting without direct orders from his boss, General Vysotsky.

The early April afternoon was sunny and 60 degrees. Elizabeth sat on a bench near the base of the monument. She wore a concealed transceiver. Lamont sat on another bench not far away. He fed birds from a paper sack with his good arm. His Glock.40 was hidden in his sling. She leaned back and closed her eyes and let the sun shine on her face.

She felt someone take a seat on the bench next to her and opened her eyes. Dimitri Yakov was about forty, of average height. His suit was tailored, English made, a gray pinstripe of fine wool. His eyes were blue, his hair a sun lit blond. He wasn't wearing a hat. Like Elizabeth, he wore his coat open to the warm weather.

"A beautiful day, Director. It can be so tiresome when the rains keep everything gray. Thank you for coming." He didn't offer a hand.

"Your note didn't say why you wanted to meet. It's unusual, to say the least."

"Something has come to our attention. My superior hopes you may shed light on it."

Right to the point.

Yakov smiled. "Did you know that we study your methods, Director? We are, you might say, admirers. Too bad you are not working for us."

"We study Zaslon as well, Dimitri. May I call you Dimitri? But you haven't asked me here to sing our mutual praises."

"Your CIA is up to something it shouldn't be." Yakov watched her.

"Oh?"

"A video was delivered to General Vysotsky. It captured a meeting featuring your Director. You are familiar with this video, by chance?"

Yakov's English felt stiff. Or perhaps it was his way of being polite. Elizabeth was certain Yakov had a side that wasn't polite at all. The video had to be the same one that had come to her. Where Lodge talked about Demeter and Russia. Should she admit she had seen it?

"Was there a man named Dansinger in this video?"

"Ah. You have seen it. Naturally, we are curious as to what is intended."

Yakov reached into his pocket. He took out a piece of paper. He handed it to her.

"This is a copy of a note accompanying the video."

Do not jump to conclusions. In this matter, the Project is with you. A friend.

"May I be frank, Director?"

"Please."

"This Demeter operation. A CIA plot against us cannot be tolerated. If this comes to the attention of certain people, it will cause very bad results. There are some who see your country as, ah, aggressive toward us. Overtly hostile, in fact."

"Go on."

"Whoever sent that video indicates your group may be of assistance. We wish to understand this. For now, General Vysotsky has chosen to keep things between our two respective organizations. He wonders what is meant by the comment that you are with us?"

Elizabeth had never been in a situation like this before. How much should she tell him? What could she tell him? SVR had seen the video. No secrets there. Yakov was right, if it reached the highest levels in the Kremlin it would make a lot of trouble.

She knew what her father would say.

Play the cards you got. Sometimes you bluff. Sometimes you don't. Winning is all about knowing when to do one or the other.

She decided not to bluff. She chose her words with care. "We are concerned about Director Lodge."

"By 'we' you refer to your group?"

"Yes."

"Who sent it?"

"I don't know. I think someone in our intelligence community."

Yakov nodded. "That is also our conclusion. You say you are concerned. What is your concern?"

"I am certain Lodge murdered Wilkinson."

"The head of BRES, in the video?"

"Yes. I think he was killed because he withdrew from whatever Lodge and Dansinger are planning. It proves Lodge is out of control, willing to do anything to avoid exposure. He's gone over the line. For us, Lodge has now become the enemy. Whatever he's doing is not sanctioned. It's not in America's interest. Or yours."

Yakov's face showed no emotion. *Don't ever play poker with this man,* she thought. Yet, here she was.

"What is Demeter?"

"We don't know yet. Now I have a question for you. Did you intervene in Bulgaria?"

"You are correct. It was one of our operatives."

"Why?"

"To be frank, that was not our original intention. Our agent followed your people, knowing Gelashvili would come after them. We wanted to, ah, remove Gelashvili. Collateral damage was not deemed important After we received the video and the note our agent was ordered to make sure no harm came to your team."

"Collateral damage? My team?" She felt the beginning of anger.

Yakov shrugged. "It is the way of our business, is it not?"

It was. She took a breath.

"Dimitri." She was about to cross a bridge. "Lodge has to be stopped. Whatever he's planning is bad for both of us. This can't be done publicly. I've alerted the President, but there's no proof of anything. He can't act without it."

"But you and I know Lodge is, how do you say, over the line. There are obvious solutions."

"This is America. I can't remove Lodge the way you removed Gelashvili. Besides, there's Dansinger. There are others. It's a conspiracy. It has to broken open."

"What do you propose?"

"Perhaps we can work together." She thought about what to say.

"This man is head of your CIA. You say you would work with us against him. Forgive me, I find this difficult to believe."

"Whoever sent us that video believes it."

"How do you see it, this working together?"

"I need a secure line of communication to Vysotsky. I want cooperation if my operatives have to enter Russian territory or spheres of influence. A guarantee nothing will be done against Lodge. Time to deal with this."

"You are asking for a lot, Director."

"I am in a much better position to do this than you are. If you practice your style of removal against Lodge it will complicate things. Leave him to me. Anything I learn about Demeter I will pass on to you."

"Your Pentagon may be involved."

"That remains to be seen. I want to be clear about something. I will do nothing to compromise our security. Be certain of that."

Lamont had stopped feeding the birds. Now he appeared to be taking a nap. He had heard every word of the conversation on his earpiece.

Yakov stood. "I will pass your proposal to General Vysotsky, Director."

As if he didn't already know, she thought. *Yakov is probably wired right to Vysotsky's office in Moscow.*

She took a card from her pocket and handed it to him. "This number is secure. It will reach me at any time."

"You will hear from us." Yakov made a slight bow and walked away.

Lamont got up and walked over.

"You think they'll cooperate?"

"I don't know. It's in their best interests."

"Never thought we'd get in bed with the Russians."

"Bad analogy, Lamont. It's a chess game, not a one night stand."

"Whatever you say, Director. As long as we're not the ones who end up getting screwed."

CHAPTER THIRTY-THREE

A silver and blue Lear Jet turned at the end of Dansinger's private runway and taxied toward a sun-baked hanger. A white limousine waited near the hanger doors. DCI Lodge gazed out the port window. The Texas panhandle stretched away into shimmering, hazy distance.

Dansinger's research compound took up several hundred acres. It was surrounded by a tall metal fence topped with razor wire. Signs picturing a red lightning bolt marked the fence at regular intervals. Rows of large, identical one story buildings marched along one side. Each was painted light tan. Each had a rounded green metal roof. A perfect grid of paved roads separated the buildings. A black security vehicle patrolled between them. It reminded Lodge favorably of a concentration camp, except the buildings concentrated plants, not people.

Harold Dansinger waited by the limo as Lodge descended from the plane. He looked tan and fit under his white Stetson.

"Wendell, good to see you. Smooth flight?"

"Very smooth, Harold, thanks. I'm looking forward to our meeting."

"I think you'll be pleased."

A driver held the door for them. They got in the back of the car. Dansinger pushed a button. An opaque partition rose behind the driver.

"We can talk freely."

"Demeter?"

"We're waiting for the spring planting to take hold. Another week or so should be about right. We monitor the area daily."

Lodge nodded. "Efficient. It's one of the things I appreciate about you, Harold."

The limo drove toward one of the buildings. Each was the length of a football field and half again as wide. The car turned right and then left. It continued toward the back of a building with a large number 1 painted on the side. The car stopped by a plain door. Lodge and Dansinger got out. Dansinger slid a card through a slotted reader and opened the door.

They entered a room like executive boardrooms everywhere, except there were no windows. A long, polished table of wood. Comfortable leather chairs. An overhead projector mounted on the ceiling. Lighting that illuminated without being intrusive. Walls papered in soothing tones. Thick carpet on the floor. A remote control rested on the table.

Dansinger walked to a large sideboard of polished oak. It was set with decanters and glasses of cut crystal.

"Drink?"

"Single malt, if you've got it. Neat."

"I'll join you." Dansinger poured the drinks. The two men sat down.

"I've prepared a short presentation for you. I thought you'd like to see Demeter in action."

He picked up the remote and pressed a button. A screen descended at one end of the room. The lights dimmed. Dansinger pressed again. The video appeared. It showed the interior of one of the large buildings and a broad field thick with green plants. Overhead, bright UV lighting simulated the sun.

"This is one of our test facilities for wheat. We have others for barley, corn, rice and millet. Also for leafy vegetables like cucumbers. The surface you see here is about one and a half acres."

"Is this one of your engineered crops?"

"No. This is natural, grown using standard methods. Just like the crops in the target area."

On screen, a man entered the room through an airlock. He wore a white hazmat suit and carried a jar with a red label. It could have been taken from the spice rack in anyone's kitchen. He uncapped it and shook some of the contents over a small area. Black specks drifted down over the young plants. He put the cap back on the jar and exited the room.

"Airborne?"

"Yes. Notice that he used a very small amount of material. Now the video will go into time lapse mode. About one minute a day. What you will see takes approximately ten days."

The frames of the video began to flicker through the first day. The lights dimmed as the cycle followed the sun. Not much happened. The plants were green and vibrant. Lodge could almost sense the life pushing up out of the soil.

The morning of the second day dawned. The plants were still green.

On the third day something had changed. A hint of yellow had appeared in the green. Plants were affected in all directions.

On the fourth day a broad swath of yellow had spread outward into the field. Patches of yellow were beginning to appear farther away. Some of the plants were turning brown.

By the fifth day, it had reached the center.

By the sixth day, the entire field was infected.

By the tenth day, the field was dead.

Dansinger used the remote to turn off the projector and raise the lighting. The screen retracted into the ceiling.

"I've been working on this for two years. The genetic code of the virus has been altered to greatly accelerate reproduction. The original virus devastated ancient Mesopotamia. That was just grains like wheat. Demeter will attack the other crops I mentioned as well. The beauty is that the virus has a finite life cycle. Once the damage is done, it dies."

"No permanent damage?"

"None. It was one of the requirements. The outbreak will begin in the Ukraine and spread throughout the old Soviet Union. I estimate two to three months before total crop failure over the entire region. There will be famine. The people will riot. Moscow will not be able to contain it and national and regional governments will collapse. Once it's over, we'll step in with food and seeds for the new crops. And, perhaps, a bit of military assistance as needed. Russia will be finished."

"Is there an antidote to this?"

"There is, stored in the Utah facility. It was another requirement. No one will be able to develop it in time."

Lodge sipped his drink. "It's too bad about Wilkinson."

"Yes. Regrettable. It was a hard decision."

The two men considered their regrettable decision for a second or two.

"Rice will have his hands full. We have a good chance of getting our man into the White House."

"You're a visionary, Harold. You should be President."

Dansinger laughed. "Oh, no. Much better to be in the shadows. It's always been that way for people like us."

He finished his drink. "You did well with those scientists, Wendell. Campbell was too close."

"Harker and her people are still looking for the urn."

"Ah, the urn. It has been in my family forever. Let them look. They'll never find out what happened to it."

"How did your family get it?"

"You know my ancestors were from Germany? Back then they lived in Erfurt. It was quite a place, one of the big medieval cities. Rigidly Catholic. The name was Danzinger back then, with a 'Z'. Anyway, there was a wave of emigration from Bulgaria around the middle of the eleventh century. Mostly Greeks who had become unpopular in the Slavic makeover of what had been Thrace. Some of them were pagans. The smart ones converted. Those who didn't were killed or driven away."

"And the urn?"

"One of my ancestors was on the town council, an influential merchant. He acquired the urn from one of the less fortunate Greeks in return for his conversion and his life."

"And it was never opened?"

"No. It amused my family to keep it sealed. Sort of a family legend. The curse of a goddess, all that. They were wealthy, they didn't need the money the gold would have brought. The urn was a powerful symbol of their wealth. Nothing clinked inside, like coins or jewels, or I'm sure it would have been opened. When they emigrated to the States, the urn came with them."

"But you got curious."

Dansinger nodded. "I knew the story, of course. I thought about it. I decided it was time to open it and see what was actually in there. It contained spores, just as Campbell suspected after he found those tablets. One thing led to another. Now we have Demeter. I'm sure the goddess would be proud."

Lodge swirled whiskey in his glass, drained it. "I've dreamed of this for years. Moscow finished for good. It will be a great day."

Dansinger reached for the bottle of single malt, poured two new drinks. He raised his glass.

"To the dream."

CHAPTER THIRTY-FOUR

Billy Elroy worked as a janitor for Dansinger Enterprises. It was a pretty good job. He had health insurance, a 401K, two weeks off a year, sick days if he needed them, and $13.50 an hour, 40 hours a week, time and a half for extra hours. Some people thought Billy wasn't the brightest bulb in the pack, but he was smart enough to know a good thing when he saw it. Working here was a good thing. He was careful about what he pilfered.

He never took anything important. An extra package or two of toilet paper. Soap. Sometimes a little food from one of the refrigerators in the lab. Billy liked a good salad with his barbecued ribs, and a lot of times he had an assortment of greens to choose from. No one ever missed a bowl of salad fixings.

Billy worked the last shift, from four in the afternoon to midnight. He liked the quiet of the big place after everyone had gone home. There were other janitors, of course. Everyone usually got together in the main cafeteria around eight for their meal break. The cafeteria was closed at night, but people brought their own food. Machines provided hot coffee, snacks and sodas, if you wanted something.

At the end of the break everyone went their own way. From meal break to quitting time, Billy worked alone. His job was building four, including the meeting rooms and the lab. Each building had it's own laboratory, where Dansinger's plant geniuses did their thing. Billy had a key card that granted access.

Billy had a regular routine. He always started with the meeting rooms. Then he'd move on to the bathrooms and halls and offices, then the lab to finish up. The lab had the refrigerators. He never had to go in the largest part of the building. Billy didn't know exactly what went on in there, except it was where they experimented with growing things. He didn't really care. He was just grateful he didn't have to clean it.

He finished ten minutes before the end of his shift, which gave him time to see if there were any goodies in the fridge. Five huge refrigerators lined one wall of the lab. He ignored the first four. They held test tubes, vials, small round dishes with weird stuff. Nothing edible. Sometimes the fifth had good things in it.

This time the fifth had nothing green. It was filled with row upon row of pepper jars filled with black grains, just like the ones in the store. They had blank red labels, waiting for whatever would identify the contents, like Cayenne or Black Pepper or Chili.

He was almost out of pepper at home. Billy liked a lot of pepper on his food. He chose a container from far in the back of the lower shelf. He opened the lid and shook a little on his hand to make sure. Fine black grains settled on his palm. He sniffed it and sneezed. Pretty fine grind, but it would do. No one would miss one jar. He put the jar in his pocket.

Time to go home. It was Friday. He had two weeks of vacation coming. Tomorrow he was headed to Nebraska to visit his brother and help with the spring planting.

CHAPTER THIRTY-FIVE

Elizabeth hadn't heard from Yakov. She was worried. What if Vysotsky went to his boss? Anything might happen then.

Stephanie came in.

"The Pentagon. I found something."

"What have you got?"

Steph sat down. "They really had this buried. That place is like a Chinese puzzle box. I had to go through four separate revolving firewalls, each one worse than the one before."

Elizabeth waited.

"They have a war game scenario called Black Harvest."

"What's it about?"

"Occupying Russia."

"You have got to be kidding."

"No. Of course it's hypothetical."

"Sure it is. Unless they decide to implement it."

"It's a detailed plan based on one key element, catastrophic crop failure across the entire country. It assumes collapse of the government, chaos and famine. That provides an opportunity to enter Russia as the good guys bringing food and relief. Of course, supplies have to be protected by troops and the logistics to back them up. The phrase they use is 'Humanitarian Advisors'."

"They do turn a good phrase, don't they. Who can argue with that?"

"There's more."

"There always is."

"Guess how they propose to restore the food supply?"

Elizabeth reached for her pen. "Seeds." She began tapping. "Dansinger."

Steph nodded.

"Any mention of Demeter?"

"No. But the association seems obvious. Demeter must be a plan to initiate the crop failure. Black Harvest is the follow up."

"Lodge and Dansinger are going to do something to cause it."

"Demeter's curse. Something that kills crops and causes famine."

Harker thought about it. "Campbell finds the reference to the urn. He doesn't know anyone has it, he just wants to find it. He also doesn't want the Pentagon to know about it. He tells two people, everyone dies."

Steph brushed a speck from her shoulder. "Dansinger and Lodge didn't want anyone following up on it. Even though it disappeared more than two thousand years ago."

"Dansinger must have it. If anyone could use old virus material to create something new it would be him. He's got brilliant geneticists working for him."

"Lodge would be able to plant those bombs. But how did he know about Campbell?"

"He must have someone at CDC, Steph. Someone working with Campbell who knew Wiesner and Campbell were working on a bio-warfare program. Or maybe someone in the Pentagon."

"It still doesn't explain Gelashvili coming after Selena in Greece."

"I think Lodge sent him. He's gone to a lot of trouble to keep everyone away from that urn. It was a mistake."

"How so?"

"If he'd stopped after he killed Campbell and the others, it would have ended there. He probably thought it would. He couldn't have known McCullough would call Selena and give her a copy of those tablets. Somehow he knew she'd talked with McCullough and got worried. By sending Gelashvili and going after us he raised the ante."

"How would he know about Selena and McCullough?"

"I don't know."

"What do we do next, Director?"

"We wait for the team to get back. And we wait to hear from Vysotsky."

CHAPTER THIRTY-SIX

Besida Gelashvili paced back and forth in Zviad's study. The day was sunny. She could see children playing in Gorky Park. Damn him. Damn all of them. Damn Iosif for getting himself killed. She couldn't gain control of the organization without him. The vultures were already circling and she was a disposable liability. She knew too much. She needed to get out of Moscow. Her daughters were young, no threat to anyone. They were safe but she wasn't. She felt her belly, where Iosif's baby was growing. She thought about what she'd take with her.

A servant came into the room. He was nervous.

"What is it?"

Before he could answer, three men entered the room. One of them held up his identification. A round, gold badge. In the center, a five pointed star surrounding a blue lined globe. A banner of red, blue and white spread under the star and globe.

SVR. Not FSB, but foreign intelligence. Besida forced herself to remain calm.

"Besida Gelashvili?"

"Yes."

"You will come with us."

"What..."

One of the men took her arm. "Shut up. Come with us."

A black Mercedes waited outside. The men pushed her into the back seat. One sat on either side. No one spoke until they reached SVR headquarters.

"Get out."

The men took her inside, down a long flight of steps, into a dingy corridor. They weren't gentle about it. One of them pulled open a door.

"In there." He shoved her into the room. The door shut behind her.

A narrow metal shelf extended from one wall. There were no blankets or sheets. There was a toilet without a seat.

It smelled of urine and shit and vomit. There was no window. The walls were concrete. There was nothing else in the room.

For the first time since she was a child, Besida felt real fear.

CHAPTER THIRTY-SEVEN

The team filled Elizabeth's office. Harker told them about the Pentagon scenario. She briefed them on the approach by Yakov. She still hadn't heard from Vysotsky.

"Now you're all up to speed. Ideas?"

"What about the President," Nick said. "Have you let him know?"

"I don't have anything to give him, no proof. He's waiting to see if I come up with something."

"He doesn't know about the Russian approach?"

"He doesn't need to know."

Lamont rubbed his arm. "Lodge was bad enough. Now it's the Pentagon?"

"We can't be certain of that. But it's likely. Maybe not official."

"Someone setting up a convenient option that just happens to be handy?"

"That's what I think. A war game scenario is only a scenario, a possibility. The Joint Chiefs wouldn't do this. They don't like Russia, but they wouldn't kill millions of people and march in with an undeclared war under the guise of humanitarian relief."

"Millions?" Ronnie said.

"If the crops fail in Russia it will cause famine." Nick tugged on his damaged ear. "They're not equipped to handle something like that. Hell, we aren't equipped for something like that. The Federation would fragment. It would be chaos. Civil war."

"Time for assumptions?" Selena looked around the room. "We've done this before. It worked out pretty well."

She seemed fine. Nick focused on the task.

"Okay. Assumption number one is that Lodge and Dansinger want to unleash a lethal crop virus against Russia soon. The spring crops are just coming up."

"How would they do it?" Lamont asked. "Get it started?"

"Probably airborne. It's the best way. Anything else would take too long."

Elizabeth made a note. Something she could give Vysotsky. If he contacted her.

"What's assumption number two?"

"Number two is someone in the Pentagon is in on this," Nick said. "We have to find out who it is."

"That won't be easy. I had a heck of a time hacking in."

"We could look for personal connections, Steph. Maybe Dansinger is buddies with someone over there. Lodge is, for sure."

Elizabeth made another note. This one wasn't for Vysotsky. She beat a short tattoo with her pen on the desktop. "The big question is how are we going to stop them? Yakov talked about removing Lodge. He meant kill him. We can't do that. We can't let the Russians do it either. If they get worried enough, they'll try."

"How come we always end up in the middle of something like this?" Lamont said.

"Because we're super heroes, Shadow." Nick smiled.

"Yeah? Where's my cape and shield?"

"Not my fault you can't find them. You had them with you, you wouldn't have gotten shot in Khartoum."

Elizabeth waved her pen in the air. "Children. Stay on task, here."

"Maybe we could get them to make a mistake." Selena smoothed a non-existent crease in her skirt.

"Go on."

"They don't know we've figured it out. That we know as much as we do."

"We don't know that, but you're probably right."

"We could let them know."

"Make them come after us?"

"Yes."

"They already did."

"That was because we were after the urn. Maybe we should keep looking for it."

"Forget the urn," Harker said. "It doesn't matter anymore. We'll assume Dansinger has it."

Ronnie said, "We can't go after Lodge, but we can go after Dansinger. Get his attention."

"I'm listening."

"He's got buildings in Texas, right?"

"Lots of them. It's where he develops his products."

"Why don't we see exactly what he's doing down there?"

"Recon," Nick said.

"Yup. Maybe a little sabotage at the same time."

"And leave a trail."

Ronnie nodded. "Something obvious. We want him to know it was us. He'd have to react. He's not going to call the cops."

"He'll probably call Lodge."

"Works for me."

"We do this, we'll stir up a hornet's nest." Harker smiled. She looked like a mischievous elf. "I like it."

CHAPTER THIRTY-EIGHT

Alexei Vysotsky considered his options. The results of Besida Gelashvili's interrogation lay on his desk. She'd been persuaded to give him enough to smash Gelashvili's gang. Russia would be a better place because of it. He had his satisfaction. Now it was up to FSB. He'd already forwarded what he wanted them to see. From here on in it was their problem.

What he hadn't wanted them to see was the connection to the Americans. Besida told him it had been an American who'd sent Gelashvili after the woman in Greece. Maybe it was Lodge. Alexei didn't know who it was and Besida was no longer available for interrogation.

He thought about Harker. Could she be trusted to go after Lodge? It was in her country's interest, as she'd pointed out to Yakov. In Russia, an agreement like that would be considered treason. Alexei knew Harker was no traitor. He admired her, what she had accomplished with her small organization. His file on the Project ran for many pages.

Her interests coincided with his own. The irony of two secretive and opposed intelligence organizations cooperating in common cause did not escape him. She had been an enemy before. She would be again. What was she now?

He thought about her conditions. He'd meet them, for now. With one addition. He wanted Korov involved. He wanted an unfiltered source on the scene. If Harker agreed, they could make a deal. It would show sincerity on her part. She wouldn't like it. If she didn't agree there were other options.

Demeter had to be uncovered and stopped. Demeter was also a golden opportunity to get inside a key American unit, to find out how they thought, to measure their capabilities, probe for weakness. If there was a god of espionage, he must be smiling. If their positions were reversed, if he were in Harker's place, he would have little choice. Exposure of the plot to the Kremlin raised the specter of nuclear war. She would have to agree.

He took out the number Harker had provided and picked up his phone.

CHAPTER THIRTY-NINE

"A Russian?" Nick was angry. "Come on, Director."

"Calm down, Nick. It's part of the deal. Gives us a chance to learn something. This man isn't just any Russian." She passed Korov's file over. "He's Zaslon. We've never gotten close to them before."

Lamont and Ronnie studied Korov's picture.

"He reminds me of my DI." Ronnie passed it to Selena.

"He's a professional. Just like the rest of you. Special Forces, lots of combat experience. He speaks English. He won't be a drag on the team."

"He's not part of the team. He's an outsider. I don't give a shit if he's Superman, it's my team. We're a family. This guy's the enemy. We don't even have a mission, yet." Carter felt his blood pressure rising. "Why do we need him tagging along? We don't have time to work this guy in. He doesn't know how we do things."

Harker's eyes tightened. "Make time, Nick. This isn't an option. As far as that goes, Major Korov is highly skilled. You might learn something."

"God damn it..."

"That's enough, Nick."

He threw up his hands in surrender. "I don't like it."

"You don't have to like it. I expect your full attention and cooperation."

"He takes orders from me."

"That's a given. For what it's worth, Korov is the one who showed up in Bulgaria. In the church."

"Mmm."

"Nick, I understand. It's unheard of. There's not much trust on either side. I have to make sure Vysotsky doesn't go to the Kremlin with that video. He has to make sure we're really going after Lodge. He's sticking his neck way out here. So am I. Korov is the deal maker."

"Does Rice know about this?"

"No."

"When does Comrade Korov get here?"

"They're not comrades anymore. Today. This evening. I booked him into the Marriott. I want you and Ronnie to meet him tomorrow and bring him here."

"You put him in a hotel? Bring him here? For Christ's sake, Director."

"Here." She gave him a hard look. "They already know where we are and who we are. He won't see anything he doesn't already know or suspect. I want you to get a sense of who he is. Bond with him."

"You want me to buy him a beer while I'm at it?"

"That's a good idea. He might prefer vodka."

Harker smiled.

"What's so funny?"

They all laughed.

"Bonding and togetherness with the Russian comrade. I'll remember this."

"I'm sure you will."

CHAPTER FORTY

Selena opened the door to her new condo. The place was empty and clean and smelled of new construction. She loved that smell. Ready for life, full of potential, a blank canvas for new possibilities. Sunlight streamed through the windows. It filled the empty rooms with light and spilled gold over the hardwood floors.

She closed the door and stood for a moment looking at the space. The kitchen opened onto the living area across a curving expanse of polished granite. It was one of the things she loved about the design. She walked across the room. Her footsteps echoed in the silence. The floor was on top of the building. Somewhere a siren wound through the streets far below and faded into the distance.

Her things from San Francisco would arrive in a few days. She hadn't had time to look for furniture yet. Selena pictured the Klee on the living room wall. Or maybe in the bedroom. She'd arranged to upgrade the alarms. A former CIA operative and friend of her uncle would take care of it.

She toured the bedrooms, the baths, came back to the kitchen. She leaned against the counter. What would it be like, living here? With Nick, if that worked out? She'd been on her own for a long time. She liked her privacy, her space. She liked doing things her own way. She liked arranging things as she pleased.

She was having strong second thoughts. Nick had done nothing about subletting his apartment. Why was she pushing it?

She opened the sleek refrigerator. It was empty except for a six pack of bottled water. She took one of the bottles and closed the door. Walked over to the counter with the bottle.

She took in the beautiful space and suddenly felt depressed. That happened a lot recently. Feeling depressed. As if all the light was leaving.

Her life had changed so much since her uncle's murder, since she'd met Nick. She could never have imagined it, not in her wildest fantasies. It was as if she'd stepped through an invisible barrier into an insane video game, where nothing was fixed and people stayed dead for real.

She didn't think much about her safety. She thought that was weird. She ought to be worried. But she wasn't. When something bad went down, she became the moment. She was the moment, doing whatever she had to do. It wasn't a conscious thing. After, she might think about what it meant, what she'd done. That was part of the problem. Nick had told her once not to think about things before they happened or much about them after. Easy for him to say. It wasn't easy for her. She didn't think it was really as easy for him as he made it out to be. Otherwise, why did he have nightmares? Now she had them too.

Maybe it was all meaningless. Maybe what she did wouldn't change anything. But if it was meaningless, she couldn't justify the deaths she caused. Not only that, she was good at killing people. It bothered her. She'd always tried to be the best at whatever she did. It carried over into killing.

In the beginning, the first time she'd killed someone, she'd felt guilty about not feeling guilty. It wasn't like that now. Now she just felt plain guilty.

Did she really love Nick? Maybe she was just hooked on his Alpha Male competence. Not to mention the sex. He took her places in bed like no one she'd slept with before. Not that she'd had many lovers, she'd never been promiscuous. Where would it go, after he moved in with her? Where would it be ten years from now?

If he's still alive. If I'm still alive. What about children?

The thought was unexpected. Unwelcome. She couldn't imagine children here. She couldn't imagine children anywhere. Her gut twisted. If she kept doing this there would never be children. Any path she walked with Nick didn't have children on it. She didn't know if she wanted children. Her mind was a stew of conflicting thoughts.

"Screw this," she said to the empty room.

She let herself out. She thought she'd have a drink somewhere. Maybe she could meet Nick for dinner and they could pretend they were like everybody else.

Normal.

CHAPTER FORTY-ONE

Nick stepped out of the entrance to his building. He was on his way to meet Selena at a restaurant near DuPont Circle. He thought about what he'd say to her. About living with her in the new condo.

A gleaming black Cadillac limo sat by the curb, motor idling. Nick recognized it as the armored Presidential model. Not something you saw every day. A $300,000 car. Five inch thick armor. Run flat tires. Turbo charged 6.6 liter diesel engine. Security countermeasures beyond most people's conception.

The windows were black. At the same time he saw the limo, he saw a man on either side of him. His hand moved toward his pistol.

"Please don't, Director Carter. You are in no danger." The man on the right had a deep voice, calm. "Someone wants to speak with you."

Both men wore dark overcoats and sunglasses and earpieces. They might have been Secret Service, but something told him these two didn't work for the Treasury Department. They kept out of reach and made no sudden moves. Their hands were outside their pockets and away from their bodies. Both men wore their hair short. Both had hard, experienced faces. Nick assessed his chances. He figured it at about 50/50 in a fight. He'd never reach the gun in time.

He stopped on the sidewalk. A driver in a dark suit got out of the car. He had sunglasses and an earpiece, like the others. He came around to the curbside and opened the rear door. Waiting.

"If someone wants to talk, why not call?" Stalling. He felt the adrenaline kick in.

"Director. I assure you, there is no harm intended." The voice of the man was educated. "If you would please get in the car."

"I have a dinner engagement."

"Ms. Connor has been advised that you will be delayed."

"And if I choose not to get in?"

"As you wish, Director. No one will attempt to force you, but you would be making a mistake." No menace in the comment, just a recitation of fact.

The car door beckoned. If they knew about Selena, knew where she was, they were efficient, organized. A possible threat if they wanted to be, maybe to Selena. Nick weighed his options, shrugged, got in the back seat of the Cadillac. Sometimes you had to go with the play. The door closed.

The windows were opaque. The interior was lit by overhead halo lighting. The back of the limo stretched comfortable and long, with the smell of new leather. The leather was black. The limo had a black glass partition in front, behind the front seat and the driver. Another partition of thick, black glass ran all along the length of the rear compartment. Nick had never seen anything like that in the back of a Cadillac. He could not see the driver, or whoever sat on the other side of the rear seat. A speaker grill was set in the glass by his head.

The car started moving, quiet, soft. Nick couldn't tell if the men had gotten into the car. He could not see outside through the black glass. The inside of the door lacked a handle. He was along for the ride until someone decided he could get out.

It was like riding in a luxurious closet. Or a coffin.

They hadn't taken his gun, but the glass was probably bullet proof. He'd end up shooting himself with the ricochet. They hadn't threatened him. That was interesting.

"I apologize for the intrusion, Director."

The voice from the speaker startled him. It was altered by electronics. It could be the voice of a man or a woman. Hell, it could be the voice of a child. Nick didn't think a child sat on the other side of that glass.

He waited. The obvious questions were unlikely to be answered.

Nick heard the person on the other side chuckle. Probably a man, he thought.

"Not curious about who I am?"

"Would it do any good to ask? Why the dramatics?"

"It seemed best this way. Appointments and phone calls are not secure. This vehicle is. May I call you Nick?"

"You can call me whatever you like. Who are you?"

"You may call me Adam."

"What do you want?"

"I sent you the video."

Nick didn't have to ask what video.

"Why send it to us?"

"Surely that's obvious. Who else could I send it to? The Pentagon? The FBI? Langley, perhaps?"

"And the Russians?"

"Vysotsky will not go to his boss. He will only do that if there is no other choice. These things can escalate out of control. Vysotsky is a patriot. He does not want a war with us that Russia can't win. There are people in the Kremlin who don't understand that concept. He can help. He will be invaluable if you have to enter Russia."

"No one's going to invite us into Russia."

"Stranger things have happened."

"What is Demeter?"

"A plan to destroy all food crops in Russia with a fast-acting virus."

"That's the conclusion we came to."

"Dansinger is an egomaniac and a fanatic. He wants Russia on its knees. He thinks he can control this virus once it is released. I think he's wrong. It is likely to spread throughout Asia. Half the world's food supply will be destroyed within a few months. Think what will happen, if he succeeds."

"How does Lodge come in?"

"He hates Russia as much as Dansinger. Among other things, he provides covert support. Wet work."

"Campbell and the others."

"Yes. He had them terminated. He has his own private unit of rogue agents operating outside the boundaries."

Nick made a mental note. Terminated.

"Dansinger is part of a very powerful organization. He has promised Lodge the White House four years from now and he can deliver it."

What Adam had just told him explained Lodge's motivation. The White House could be delivered. Nick didn't want to believe that, but somehow he did.

"What organization?"

"We'll talk about that on a different day."

The car rolled through the streets. Nick had no idea where he was. Sometimes they stopped, he assumed for lights or traffic. Sometimes they turned.

The electronic voice was unsettling. "Lodge has been observing everyone in the Project for some time. Did you know he had someone outside your cabin in California the last time you were there?"

Son of a bitch, Nick thought. He kept silent.

"He had someone watching when you and Doctor Connor met with McCullough. I assume he sent those Georgian gangsters to Greece."

"You seem to know a lot about Lodge. Why haven't you stopped him?"

"We're doing what we can."

Nick noted the plural. We.

"Is the Pentagon part of this?"

"We think there is a rogue element in the military leadership. Dansinger is involved in a Pentagon bio-warfare program. He receives a great deal of money from them. His research facilities and laboratories are unmatched, except at CDC."

We, again.

"Why are you telling me this?"

"Demeter is about to be implemented. That must not happen. The virus is stockpiled in Building Four at

Dansinger's Texas research facility. It has to be destroyed and your group can do it."

"You want to use us. Why should we cooperate?"

"Because it is in the country's best interest to do so."

Nick said nothing.

"One thing you should know. The virus is airborne. You can't blow it up. Use thermite charges. Intense heat will finish it."

"What does the virus look like?"

"Demeter looks exactly like common pepper. Samples are kept in one of the refrigerators in the laboratory. The main supply is in a large freezer, packed in sealed boxes. All of that is in Building Four."

The car slowed.

"One more thing." The electronic voice crackled over the speaker. "He has effective security on site. Be careful."

The car stopped. The door opened. They were in front of the restaurant.

"How do I contact you?"

There was no response. Nick got out. The driver closed the door, went around the back, got in. The car drove away. The license plate was obscured.

He walked into the restaurant where Selena waited.

CHAPTER FORTY-TWO

April in Washington. The day was sunny and warm, in the high 60s. Ronnie had shifted to summer mode. He wore a bright blue Hawaiian shirt with surfboards all over it, green Dockers and a tan linen jacket that concealed his Glock. He'd gone for Oakley wraparounds and a hat that would have pleased Frank Sinatra. Winter, Ronnie dressed dull. The sun brought out another side of him.

Ronnie and Nick waited for Korov in front of the Marriott. He came out of the entrance and headed straight for them. They would have guessed what Korov did for a living even if they didn't already know.

"He's armed." Ronnie gestured. "Figures. Probably diplomatic pouch."

"He's got the look."

"Yeah he does."

Korov stopped in front of them. He was about the same height as Nick, about the same weight. He had the same tension in the way he moved. Something about the eyes said this man didn't miss much.

"So. You are Carter and Peete." He didn't offer to shake hands.

"Car's over there." They walked to Ronnie's black Hummer and got in. No one spoke on the drive to Virginia.

In the parking lot Korov eyed the anonymous gray office building that housed the Project. Noted the antennas clustered on the roof.

"You have added a few." Nick and Ronnie glanced at each other. Game on. They walked to the entrance.

"You'll have to leave your weapon at the door. You'll get it back when you leave."

"And yours?"

"I work here. I get a pass."

Korov shrugged. He took the Drotik from his holster and handed it to the security guard.

"That what you used in Bulgaria?" Ronnie studied the odd pistol.

"It is."

"Maybe you could show it to us later."

"Of course. Now that we are working together."

They got in the elevator. Half way up, Nick pushed the stop button.

"Before we go in. Neither one of us is happy about this."

Korov nodded.

"This is my team. You take orders from me. Understood?"

"Of course. We are both professionals. I read your file, Carter. We have much in common."

Nick wasn't surprised there was a file about him somewhere in Moscow.

"We need to make this work. I'm going to try. How about you?"

For the first time Korov smiled. "Honesty is good. Yes. I will try."

"Good enough." Nick pushed the button again. The elevator rose.

Selena, Stephanie and Lamont waited with Elizabeth in Harker's office. No one got up as Korov came in.

"Major Korov. I am Director Harker. Please sit down." She indicated a chair. She didn't introduce the others. Nick and Ronnie sat down on the couch.

"Getting crowded in here," Lamont said. Harker gave him a warning look.

"What are your instructions, Major? We'd all like to know."

"My orders are to cooperate with you in every way. I am to place myself under your command for the duration of this assignment. General Vysotsky showed me the video of your CIA Director."

"Then you understand our concern."

"I do. We have a mutual goal."

"How do you feel about being here? Working with us?"

"I'll be blunt. I have mixed feelings." Korov's English was excellent. "I never expected to work with Americans. I was raised to see your country as the enemy. As you were regarding the Motherland."

She opened a folder on her desk. Turned it so Korov could see. His picture was prominent. The folder contained a full history. Family, education, military service. The date he'd been recruited to Spetsnaz. His assignment to the non-existent Zaslon. Commendations for heroism under fire. Evaluations from superior officers.

If Korov was surprised, he gave no sign.

Harker closed the folder. "Your record speaks for itself. You have the skills. My question to you is if you can give us your total commitment."

"I've been ordered to do so."

"That's not what I asked."

"I will do my best."

Harker waited for the others.

"We spoke in the elevator," Nick said. "I'm willing to put him in the loop."

"Likewise." That was Ronnie.

"Selena?"

"Yes." She watched Korov. A flicker of surprise on his face.

"Lamont?"

He shrugged. "Okay."

Stephanie nodded.

"All right. That's settled."

Korov knew what had happened. He just hadn't expected it.

"If one of you had said no, would I now be on my way back to Moscow?"

"You would."

"This will be interesting."

Nick couldn't resist. "You can count on it."

CHAPTER FORTY-THREE

"Tell them about Adam, Nick."

"Who's Adam?" Lamont asked.

He briefed them, leaving out the part about the Pentagon. It was up to Harker to tell Korov or not. Nick had given her the full story earlier.

"You have no idea who Adam is?" Harker said.

"No. Whoever he is, he's got power, he's got money and he's playing his cards very close. The voice was disguised. I think Adam is a man. Just something in the way he spoke. I could have refused to get in the car. Nothing would have happened."

"You sensed no threat?"

"No."

"Do you think he was giving you accurate information about Demeter?"

"Yes."

Korov said, "I will have to pass this to Vysotsky."

"You can call him now, if you like."

"Here? Right now?"

"Yes. I told Yakov I'd let Vysotsky know immediately if we learned what Demeter was."

Korov nodded. "You continue to surprise me. You have the number?"

She picked up her phone, dialed. A short pause while the signal relayed across the world. In Moscow, Vysotsky picked up.

"Da."

"General, this is Director Harker. Major Korov would like to speak with you."

Elizabeth smiled inside. She didn't think Vysotsky would have expected that. She handed the phone to Korov.

"I will speak in Russian."

"Feel free."

Korov began talking. Selena listened. She spoke Russian. If Korov knew it, he didn't care. He paused, listened. He said

"Da" several times. Even Nick knew that meant yes. Korov gave the phone back to Harker.

"He wants to speak with you."

Harker put the call on speaker. She'd decided full transparency might build trust. She wanted Korov to see she played it straight.

"Director Harker. We meet, so to speak. What do you intend to do?" Vysotsky's English was accented but quite good.

"Now that we know what and where it is, we are going to destroy Demeter."

"Time is running out." The speaker hissed in the background. "When do you plan this operation?"

"Two nights from now. I need to get the logistics together and the team on site."

"What about Lodge?"

"Our primary concern is Demeter. After we take care of that, then Lodge."

"Major Korov will be part of the strike unit?"

"Definitely. His experience will be valuable. There may be resistance."

"Arkady is used to that." A pause. "Good hunting."

Elizabeth set the phone down.

"Let's talk about the mission. Steph, bring up the objective."

Steph tapped keys at her console. A live satellite picture came up on the big wall screen.

Harker swiveled toward the monitor. "This is Dansinger's compound in Texas. He grows experimental crops in those large buildings."

The live satellite picture was stationary, clear and detailed. A state highway paralleled the complex to the north. A straight, blacktop road ran south for about a quarter of a mile from the highway to the main gate of the compound. The compound itself was several hundred acres in size, rectangular, with the long sides on the east and west. The entrance by the gate was the only way in.

A high fence went completely around the property. Low shrubs and landscaping split the center of the compound east and west. Looking south from the highway, there were ten large buildings to the west, spaced evenly in two rows along the fence.

On the eastern side was an L-shaped building with parking areas. South of the structure, five two-story buildings followed a perfect line. It reminded Nick of a military base. A good sized airstrip ran along the eastern border, with two runways crossing each other in an offset X. It was contained within the fenced perimeter. It featured a windsock, a hanger and a helicopter pad. The pad was empty.

A paved two lane access road connected everything in a neat grid. Two more of the big buildings sat at the far eastern corner of the compound. Beyond them and the fence, the Texas panhandle headed south toward civilization.

"The outside fence is twelve feet high and electrified." Harker traced it with a laser pointer. "Razor wire on top. Floodlights that come on at dusk."

"Typical," Lamont said.

"How's your arm?"

"Better." He held it up, out of the sling. "I can use it. I've been working it."

"Good. Because you're going."

"All right." Lamont grinned. "Back in the saddle."

"There's only the one gate, backed by the guard house. Dansinger owns the land up to the highway and 5000 surrounding acres. Security will have monitors on everything. There are cameras along the outer fence and on the corners and entrances of each building. Those big buildings are where he grows his crops."

"What's that L-shaped one?" Nick said.

"That's admin. Offices. The next two buildings are for equipment, supplies, vehicle storage, that kind of thing. There's a full garage and shop. He's got a fire station with two engines. The security vehicles park there. They use GMC Suburbans, like the Feds."

Nick pointed. "Next to the Suburbans. Get a closer look."

Steph zoomed in with the satellite camera.

"Well, well. Three Humvees, M-240s on top. Early models, looks like. There's no protection for the gunner. How the hell does Dansinger have stuff like that? What's he need them for?"

"Coyotes, maybe," Ronnie said.

"That building next to them could be a barracks. Adam mentioned security."

"How many men, you think?"

Nick thought about it. "Hard to say. Three Humvees, eight SUVs. Probably two men in the guardhouse, two in the patrol vehicles. Probably three shifts. I'd guess around forty. Former military, with those Humvees and guns. Gone over to the Dark Side. That's a lot of firepower to protect a few rows of corn. He's got himself a little army there."

"Mercenaries." Korov's voice was full of contempt.

"Yeah, mercs. Except we don't call them that anymore. Now they're contractors."

"The compound is self sufficient except for power. It comes in from the road." Harker used a laser pointer to indicate an electrical substation where the access drive made a T with the highway.

"He has to keep those buildings cool." Nick studied the image. Propane tanks and gas pumps were visible in the photo.

"Those are backup generators behind that last building, near the propane tanks. Big ones. It would take a few minutes to get them up and running if the power goes down. They're vulnerable from the rear."

Two men came out of the building next to the Humvees. One man carried an assault rifle. They climbed into one of the security vehicles.

"Not much cover," Ronnie rubbed his chin. The land around the compound was featureless.

"Nothing except jack rabbits, weeds and cactus," Harker said. "Steph, show us Texas."

A map of Texas appeared on the wall monitor. Dansinger's compound was northwest of Amarillo, off Highway 87 and a state highway linking two small towns.

"I can get you and your gear to Dyess in Abilene or Sheppard in Wichita Falls. You'll have to drive from there. We can't use helicopters for this."

"Looks like Sheppard and Dyess are about the same distance away." Nick studied the map. "The roads are more direct from Sheppard. 287 to Amarillo, then 87 north. Piece of cake. Get us to Sheppard."

CHAPTER FORTY-FOUR

Nick poured wine for Selena, whiskey for himself. They sat at the counter in his apartment. He'd fixed a simple plate of snacks. Crackers, celery and cream cheese. Olives. Brie.

There was a comfortable silence between them.

"I've been thinking."

"About what?" He cut a piece of brie, smeared it on a cracker.

"Us. You and me." She sipped. "You want to move in together or not?"

There it was.

"Mostly."

"Mostly?"

"It might be a bad idea."

"Why?"

"I'm afraid I'll fuck it up."

"Me too."

"That I'll fuck it up?"

"That we both will. Maybe we should wait a little."

"You want some distance?"

"No, that's not it. I'm having a little trouble right now. With what we do. What I do."

"I know."

"I'm having nightmares. I think maybe I need to see someone."

"A shrink?"

"Or a therapist. Someone to help me sort it out. I'm having these dreams, someone's trying to kill me. I can't see who they are."

"Doesn't surprise me. I thought it would happen before now."

"What do you mean?"

"Everyone gets bad dreams who does things like we do. Soldiers, cops. Everyone. Except the psychos who love it."

"That's what bothers me. Part of me loves it." She picked up a cracker, nibbled it.

"That's because of the rush. Being on the edge. At risk. Am I right?"

She nodded.

"It's not the same thing as enjoying it the way the nut jobs do."

"So why the dreams?"

"When I came back from Afghanistan." He stopped.

"After the grenade."

"Yes. They made me talk to a shrink. We talked about this. It's called cognitive dissonance. The mind sets up a conflict between belief and reality."

"I know about that."

"We're brought up that killing people is wrong. Then we kill people. We believe we shouldn't do it. Reality is different." He shrugged. "Cognitive dissonance."

"So we get nightmares."

"Yup. PTSD is a nice catch all for a lot of different ways it shows up. Dreams is one of them."

"Doctor Nick. I still think I need a shrink."

"Maybe." He set his glass down. "I've got an idea for short term therapy."

"What about living together?"

"Why don't we talk about that later? After our therapy session?"

He took her hand and led her into the bedroom.

"Doctor Nick," she said.

CHAPTER FORTY-FIVE

Early next morning the team and Korov gathered around a flat table covered with satellite photos of the compound.

Nick began. "Harker's got the logistics locked down. Transport to Sheppard. Vehicles waiting for us there. That's the easy part. Steph dug up info on the opposition. They provide hard core security in Iraq and Afghanistan. There have been incidents with this group."

"What kind of incidents?" It was Selena.

"They shoot first and ask later. All combat vets, former Rangers, Marines, SOCOM. We have to assume they know what they're doing and will respond rapidly."

"They gotta be there to protect Demeter," Ronnie said.

"No other reason I can think of."

"Our weapons?"

"We'll take all that with us, Korov. MP-5s, side arms, grenades, ammo. Night scopes. You know the MP-5?"

The Russian nodded. "A good choice."

"We'll take Thermate-TH3 for the meltdown and C-4 just in case. All our personal combat gear. Vests and the like. Lamont, can you handle a rifle with that arm?"

"Yeah, with a bipod and a rest. Don't think I'd be much good in a running firefight, though."

"I'm thinking we take a Barrett .50 and give you an M4 for backup. You stick with the vehicles, set up and give us cover while we go in."

"That'll work."

Nick put his finger on the electrical substation at the junction of the highway and the access road.

"A big transformer fire will make a nice diversion. We'll take it out with a delayed charge and be in position when the lights go out. I'm betting they'll think it's a normal power failure. These guys have been sitting on their ass in the middle of nowhere for months with nobody shooting at them. They'll be dull. That will change pretty quick once they realize we're inside."

Selena said, "How do we go over the fence?"

"We don't go over it. We go through it with a plasma cutter. Easier and faster that way." He tapped the photo. "Here. In the rear, away from the guard shack and the barracks. Once we're in, we've got cover between the buildings. We'll get close before the power goes off."

Korov nodded.

Nick continued. "They won't see us. There's no moon. Weather says clouds, so no stars either. It'll be black as Hitler's heart out there. We'll approach from the back, beyond the lights. Lamont will set up to cover us with the Barrett. We crawl up close and go through the fence when the power goes down."

"And if the lights come back on while we're doing that?" Selena asked.

Nick was in leader mode. "We deal with it."

"Which building is the primary objective?" Korov studied the photo.

"Building Four. This one."

Building Four was in the second from the last row, in the back of the complex. That made it a little easier.

"Korov, what's your experience with demolition?"

"Extensive. I am familiar with thermite and with your detonators and explosives."

"Figures. Okay, you and I will go inside and set charges. Ronnie, you and Selena outside to cover us with Lamont as backup."

"What does this stuff look like?"

"Pepper, Ronnie. Just like pepper."

"Getting out?" Korov said. "The power will be back on with the fence."

"Lamont will take out the generators with the .50 when we're ready to leave. No need for quiet by then."

"When do we go in?"

"0300 hours. This whole thing depends on getting in without being seen. If they see us we're looking at a heavy firefight with some very pissed off people. But they're rusty. We're not."

"Forty of them?"

"Yep."

"Maybe ten to one odds," Ronnie said. "Makes it an equal fight."

CHAPTER FORTY-SIX

"Be a good crop, this year. Better than last," Bob said.

Winter wheat laid a fresh green carpet across the Nebraska prairie. Billy Elroy and his brother Bob stood on the edge of the fields. Bob had 2000 acres in wheat and corn, handed down by hard work through five generations. Billy had come to help with the spring corn planting. Disking, fertilizing, getting the machinery ready.

Billy was in awe of Bob's success. His brother had the gift for growing things. Billy couldn't grow weeds if he tried. He had tried. Everything he planted behind his house died. Finally he'd given it up.

"You going for the Ethanol thing with the corn?"

"Nah. Too damn much paperwork. My corn's for people. I got no interest in feeding cars." Bob glanced at the sun. "Getting close to dinner. Mae's got a big salad for you. She knows you like that rabbit food."

Billy grinned. "Hey, you throw enough stuff in it, it's good. I even brought the pepper." He pulled a glass jar from his pocket.

"Almost forgot about it. Here 'ya go." He tossed it over to his brother. Bob grabbed and missed. The bottle shattered on a rock. A fine cloud lifted into the air and drifted toward the field.

"Damn it, Billy." He reached down and picked up the pieces of broken glass. "You're lucky we got plenty. Come on, Mae's waiting."

The two brothers headed toward the house.

A gentle breeze blew the contents of the broken jar into the corner of the wheat field.

CHAPTER FORTY-SIX

The Texas night was blacker than the inside of the Titanic. Behind them, the flat dirt and rock of the panhandle vanished in darkness. The compound looked like an alien installation on the surface of the moon, all reflections and angles and geometric shapes of metal in the glare of the lights.

The night was cool. Nick sweated inside the black gear they all wore. Aside from their weapons, Nick and Korov carried backpacks loaded with the explosives and detonators. Everyone wore red goggles against the glare from the lights.

Their SUVs were invisible, parked beyond the wall of light. Lamont had the Barrett laid across one of the hoods, a scoped M4A beside it. He had a wide view of the compound interior. There was a clear field of fire down the security road between the buildings. He could move right as needed to cover the eastern half of the compound. For the .50 caliber Barrett and scope, distance was no problem. He had plenty of ammo. He'd be fine, as long as he didn't have to pick up the thirty pound rifle and run with it. Nick knew Lamont would do it if he had to, weak arm or not.

They waited for the substation to blow. Nick glanced at Korov, lying next to him. He seemed relaxed. Nick had to give the guy credit, he was a pro. He knew what he was doing. You could tell. They'd fallen into an uneasy acceptance of each other, masked by needle jabs of humor. Grudgingly, Nick was beginning to like the guy. Too bad he was a Russian.

"One minute." He spoke softly into his headset. They waited.

Beyond the compound, a muffled boom. The floodlights died. They pulled off the red lenses.

"Go."

They got to their feet and ran to the fence. Ronnie took out the plasma cutter. It was about the size of an electric drill, a masterpiece of military technology. It had a self-contained power supply good for eight minutes. Ronnie pulled welding goggles over his eyes. He fired the torch.

Plasma cutters used a high voltage circuit to create a small, stable pocket of plasma gas. The main plasma cutting arc ignited when brought into contact with metal. The cutting arc put out 25,000 degrees. It was bright, a necessary risk. They could be spotted, but Nick figured everyone would be busy looking at the fireworks out on the highway.

In less than a minute and a half, Ronnie had cut a door sized opening in the wire. He dropped the cutter and the goggles. They entered the compound and ran for Building Four. They reached the entrance, a recessed doorway halfway down the side. There was a camera over the door. Ronnie sprayed the lens with black.

Any patrol coming would appear to the north or south along the road.

"Selena, cover north. Ronnie, you take south." She ran across to the next building and ducked into the doorway, reached up and sprayed the camera.

Korov placed a charge against the door lock on Building Four. It went off with a dull thump. They pushed the door open, stepped inside and closed it. They turned on lights mounted on the sides of their helmets.

They were in a long corridor with a door at the end. A door in the wall led into a room with an airlock. From outside came the rumble of diesel engines starting up. A row of lights came on in the hallway.

Korov and Carter ran to the end of the hall and opened the door. They entered a modern laboratory. Tables, microscopes, centrifuges. Things Nick couldn't indentify. A row of refrigerators on one wall. Korov opened them. The last one contained glass jars filled with the virus. Korov began placing charges. Nick went to the back wall. He tried the handle on the freezer door.

Locked.

He shaped charges around the lock and hinges, set detonators and moved away.

Korov never glanced up when it blew. The door fell onto the floor. Cold air rushed into the room. Sealed boxes filled the freezer, each about two feet long and a foot high. Nick pulled off his pack and began.

The heat from the charges would melt the steel walls of the freezer and its contents along with the supporting beams of the roof. The thermite might explode as it mixed with vapor from the freezer. Adam had warned about explosions, but there wasn't anything Nick could do about it. If it did blow, the heat ought to take care of it. He hoped.

"Done." Korov came over. He helped Nick finish the sequence.

Nick activated the timers. "Ten minutes. Time to boogie."

"Boogie?"

"Get out of here."

"Nick." Selena's voice sounded in his headset. "Patrol. Coming from the north."

"Don't engage unless they spot you."

"Roger."

"I think," Korov said, "that now it gets interesting."

CHAPTER FORTY-SEVEN

Selena watched a black Suburban drive between the buildings, shining a spotlight into the shadows. The light swept back and forth across the road. She raised her MP-5, risked a quick look through the night scope and focused on the windshield in front of the driver. He had a microphone to his mouth. Her heart began pounding.

Steady your breathing. Relax. Slow your heart rate, take up the slack. Take your time. Don't fire until you have to.

Easy, standing on a firing range. Not so easy when the adrenals began pumping. She ducked back into the doorway. Across the way, Ronnie waited. Nick and Korov emerged behind him. The spotlight found them. She leaned out of the doorway and put eight rounds into the windshield of the SUV. The stuttering ripple of shots broke the silence.

The light went out. The windshield shattered. The Suburban skewed left and rammed into the side of a building. The passenger door opened and a man rolled out into the street. He had an M-16. He brought it up and fired, the bullets slamming into the wall above her head. The MP-5 bucked against her shoulder and Selena shot him, three rounds, center of the body.

A loud, shrieking alarm began. The sound came from everywhere, echoing down the space between the buildings, bouncing from the walls, filling the night air.

Nick spoke into his microphone. "That tears it. Back to the vehicles."

"Nick." Lamont's voice on the headset. "They're piling out of the barracks. One Humvee pulling out already, man on the gun. They're scrambling. Get your ass out of there."

"Take out the generators and the propane tanks."

"Roger that."

The generators were big, but they were essentially diesel engines. A few rounds through the radiators and the block would put them out of action. The unmistakable sound of the .50 boomed loud in the Texas night. They ran for the fence.

The lights flickered. The Barrett had a ten round magazine. Nick heard two more fast shots. Half the lights died.

They reached the last row of buildings before the fence. A Humvee wheeled around the corner at the far end and turned onto the road between the buildings. The gunner up top cut loose with the belt fed machine gun. The M240 spit out 7.62mm rounds, lots of them. Selena and Ronnie went right, Nick and Korov left, behind the buildings on either side of the road. They heard the whine of differentials as the vehicle powered nearer. Once it emerged from between the buildings and passed the corner, someone would get killed.

"Cover me," Korov said.

Nick didn't argue. He leaned around the corner and began firing at the gunner. "'Selena, Ronnie, cover," he yelled.

The MP-5s put out a lot of firepower. Rounds bounced from the armored vehicle, starred the windshield. The gunner ducked down, firing blind at them. Korov sprinted down the side of the building. The Humvee passed him. He leapt up onto the side as it went by and shot the gunner. He dropped a grenade through the open hatch and jumped off. The explosion blew the doors open. It slowed and stopped. Flames rose from the wreckage.

The Barrett boomed in the night. The compound went dark. It boomed again. A propane tank exploded, painting everything with yellow orange light. They ran to the end of the building. The fence was fifty yards away over open ground.

Headlights bounced toward them.

"Lamont, what do you see?"

"Looks like six, no, seven trucks. The trucks are splitting up. They're going to flank you. One Humvee headed right for you. They had some kind of trouble with the other. About four hundred yards."

"Get the RPG. Take out that bastard."

"Roger that."

"We can't outrun those trucks." Ronnie watched the headlights drawing closer.

"We have cover here," Korov said. "More or less."

"Right. Korov, you and Selena take that end. Selena, do what Korov says. Ronnie and me here. Let Lamont worry about the Humvee. We focus on the trucks. We stop them, they have to come after us on foot. Go."

Korov and Selena ran for the other side of the building. They reached the end.

"I will go high. You stay low."

Do what he says.

She crouched and peered around the corner. Above her, Korov took his stance. Three trucks were barreling toward them. They'd left the road and fanned out across the flat dirt.

"Now."

They began firing.

Selena targeted the truck to the far right. A steady stream of empty casings spewed from her gun. She watched the headlights shatter. The front tires blew out. The truck swerved and stopped. She could hear doors open, men cursing. She turned her attention to the second truck. Korov had hit the third. Flames shot up as she watched.

Somewhere in her mind Selena heard Nick and Ronnie firing at the other end of the building. She ejected an empty magazine, slammed in another, charged the weapon, began shooting. The MP5 felt like it was part of her, a live thing in her hands. Above her, Korov kept up a steady stream of fire. The air smelled of gunpowder and brass.

The lights went out on the remaining truck. It stopped.

The charges in Building Four ignited in a white hot flare of heat and light. It felt like someone had sucked all the sound away, then thrown a match into a giant pool of gasoline. There was a loud *wumpf* that shook the ground. She felt a rush of heated air. An enormous fireball of red and orange bloomed in the night. It rose and lit the compound with a hellish glare. In the sudden light she saw men running toward her. Her MP-5 was hot in her hands. She inserted another magazine. Men died in front of her.

She saw the second Humvee coming. Bullets hammered the side of the building over her head.

Korov touched her shoulder. "We fall back. To the others."

They ran toward the others. The Humvee turned the corner. Selena saw the machine gun turning toward her, bright muzzle flashes, each a messenger of death. Something dark moved through the air and the vehicle exploded. Lamont had come through with the RPG. A man wrapped in flames stumbled out of the wreck and fell screaming onto the road. Korov shot him.

"Men coming." Korov gestured over his shoulder. The light from the blazing building cast a bright red glow. Ronnie fired at shapes in the darkness. Muzzle flashes answered, winking at them in the night. They heard Lamont's M4. Steady, three round bursts.

Nick's voice on their headsets. "If they get between us and the fence, we're screwed. We run for it. Lamont, we're coming in."

"Roger."

"Now."

They sprinted for the opening in the fence. M-16s chattered behind them. Dirt flew around their feet.

Ten yards from the fence Ronnie went down. He cried out, once.

No one spoke. Korov and Nick lifted him, each on one side. They started again for the fence. Something hit Nick in his back like a hammer and he went to the ground, taking Korov and Ronnie with him. Ronnie cried out again. Nick got to his feet. They dragged Ronnie through the fence. Selena ran backwards behind them, firing at their pursuers. Lamont kept up covering fire from the truck. Spent casings littered the ground around him.

They heaved Ronnie into the back of the truck. Korov clambered in beside him. For a big man, he moved fast. Lamont fired a last burst and climbed in on the other side.

Nick got behind the wheel and started the engine. Selena scrambled into the passenger side. A window shattered. More rounds punched into the truck, hard, metallic sounds. He gunned the Suburban and headed away from the compound and hoped nothing hit the gas tank. The rear view mirror filled with bright spots like deadly fireflies in the night. Behind them, Building Four burned with sullen ferocity. Smaller fires marked the vehicles they'd destroyed.

Nick drove into the dark and prayed he didn't run into a wash or a stand of cactus. When he figured they were far enough away he turned on the lights. He pictured the map of Texas in his mind and drove across the plain, headed for the nearest road. They'd left the second vehicle, the Barrett, the launcher. Sooner or later Lodge and Dansinger would figure it out.

His back was numb. His arms didn't work as well as he would have liked. Nick heard Korov in the back seat.

"You were shot. Are you wounded?"

"I'll be okay. The vest stopped it. Thirty layers of Kevlar, it'll stop a .308. Usually. Felt like Barry Bonds slugged me with his bat. Lamont, How's Ronnie?"

"I've got the bleeding stopped. He took one in his right leg. Got the bone."

"Conscious?"

A hoarse croak from the back seat. "Yeah, I'm conscious. Hurts some."

"Run faster next time."

"Speak for yourself, Kemo Sabe." Ronnie turned to Korov. "Thanks for dragging me out of there."

Korov shrugged. "You would have done the same, nyet? It is what we do."

Ronnie nodded. "Yeah. It's what we do."

The Texas night stretched ahead of them. A rabbit darted away in the lights.

CHAPTER FORTY-EIGHT

Wendell Lodge was enraged. He was dismayed. It was bad that the stockpile of the virus had been destroyed, but it was only a setback. In the end, an annoying inconvenience. More could be produced. There would always be crops.

The fact Demeter had been discovered was what dismayed him. It was the rest of it that enraged him. He'd traced the vehicle left behind to Sheppard AFB. From there he'd followed the trail to a dead end. The RPG launcher was standard military issue. The plasma cutter found near the fence was not standard issue. Few could get their hands on that. The heavy Barrett rifle was another sign of professionals. Who had the capability, the balls, to do something like this? An all out assault on American soil?

Lodge knew. He felt the rage building. The President's pet covert ops team, Harker and her Project. It was just the kind of thing they were good at. No one else would dare. Harker was always meddling. She'd meddled in the wrong place this time. He would put an end to her interference once and for all. She was playing hardball. Two could play that game. But he needed to be careful.

Lodge swiveled around in the red leather executive chair he favored and studied the view through the French doors of his study. It was a fine morning, a pleasant view, the Virginia countryside green with spring. Dogwoods bloomed on the landscaped rolling lawn in back of his colonial home. Ordered flowerbeds shouted with color. Normally the view pleased him. Not today.

In the closed world of the CIA, no one rose to his level by accident. Lodge was, after all, a spy. He thought like a spy. He understood the game, how it worked. He had resources Harker didn't know about.

Someone had tipped her off. There weren't many who could have done that. Lodge was certain she could not have found out about Demeter in any other way. The deaths of Campbell and the others and the events in Greece had sent her after the urn. But she could never have discovered Dansinger's involvement or Demeter without help.

He would find out how she knew and plug the leak. He would take her and her team of trouble makers out of the picture for good. A plan began to form in his mind. The close bonding of the members of Harker's team was a weak spot, a vulnerability. He could exploit that vulnerability and use it to destroy them. He'd start with the weakest link.

Lodge had been waiting for this for a long time.

CHAPTER FORTY-NINE

Bob Elroy was worried sick. Something was wrong with the wheat. He and Billy had worked all morning on the machinery back at the barn. Now they stood by the fence, looking at the fields. Four days ago the wheat had been green and healthy.

Things had changed. Long patches of sickly yellow and brown fanned out into the crop. It kept spreading, whatever it was. He'd put in a call to the local office of the USDA. Someone was coming out today.

"Shit, Bob. Don't look good."

"I can't figure it. It's not insects. More like some kind of blight. There's never been anything like that around here."

"The USDA guy will know what it is."

"I guess so. Even if they've got something to stop it, it looks like I'll lose half the crop."

"You got insurance, don't you?"

"Yeah, but not enough if I lose it all. And the bank won't give me a break."

"That's for sure."

Like everyone he knew, Bob walked a fine line between profit and loss, survival and bankruptcy. The bank ruled his life, and the less said about it the better. It used to be different, back when things had been local, run by people who understood what farming was about. But then the economy tanked. His community bank was gobbled up by one of the big corporations. Now decisions about his life were made by people thousands of miles away who'd never been closer to a farm than a supermarket. It was hard enough being a farmer, what with the weather and pests and cost of things like diesel and fertilizer and insect control. Now this.

Bob didn't want to admit it, but the hollow feeling in his stomach felt like fear. Fear for his livelihood. Fear for Mae and his kids. Fear he would lose everything.

The day was crisp and sunny. A fresh, strong breeze blew across the Nebraska plains. Bob's land was in the heart of America's bread basket. Fields of wheat and corn spread for a hundred miles in every direction. Winter crops coming up, crops being planted. An ancient cycle, one he understood.

Bob loved his life. He loved farming. He thought few things were more beautiful than the silent fall of snow covering the fields during the winter, or watching towering clouds and lightning build on the far horizon in the heat of summer. Listening to the crops rustle in the wind. For Bob, amber waves of grain was a lot more than a line in a song. It was the American dream come true.

The spreading darkness in his fields was a different kind of dream, an American nightmare.

CHAPTER FIFTY

AEON meant forever.

400 years before, AEON had been born in the political unease of eighteenth century Europe.

AEON had always been about the accumulation of wealth. With wealth came power. With power came control. With control came more power, more wealth and the ability to shape the destiny of nations. With the ability to shape nations came the plan.

The ideology embraced by AEON was the ideology of power. Democracy or Fascism, right or left, it was all the same. Over the centuries AEON had learned how to manipulate them all. Political systems were merely a means to increased wealth and the creation of rigid economic separation between worker units and rulers.

The goal was in sight. The infrastructure to identify, track and contain dissidents, the corruption of government agencies across the world, the control of world finances, all were in place. Demeter and Black Harvest were the opening gambit in the final implementation of the plan.

The council had nine members, held to strict rules of accountability. There were two Americans, one member from the UK, and one each from France, China, Germany, Russia, Brazil and Japan. Meetings were held by teleconference via state of the art encrypted technology. The criterion of success was rigidly applied to each member. Mistakes were not excused and meant expulsion with unpleasant results.

Harold Dansinger was the newest member of the inner circle. He was still on probationary status. He could express his view, but could not vote when decisions were made.

The raid in Texas was a personal disaster. Dansinger needed to reassure the others that things could be brought under control and that exposure was not a remote possibility. He needed to reassure them that he himself was not a liability.

Malcolm Foxworth was the member from England. Foxworth owned a media empire that encircled the globe. Foxworth was the Supreme Leader of AEON, but he preferred the title of Chairman. It was so much more democratic sounding.

Foxworth began. "Harold, help us understand the current situation, why don't you?" Members of the Council were always addressed by their first names. It created an illusion of equality.

"As you know, Malcolm, the stockpile of Demeter was destroyed. The raid was carried out by a black ops unit called Project. It reports to the President only."

Foxworth's face hardened. "We know about the Project. They created a problem for us not long ago."

Dansinger wanted to guide their thoughts away from himself. "The actions of DCI Lodge resulted in their interest and involvement."

There was no visible reaction by Foxworth. Dansinger continued.

"I have restarted production of Demeter in the Utah facility. Stockpiles will be renewed within two months."

He sipped water. The others watched from the screens.

"What about the outbreak in Nebraska?" It was the other American member. "How did this happen? That was not part of the original plan. What do you intend to do?"

"I have not yet discovered how Demeter was released, but I believe the outbreak can work to our advantage. We simply alter the sequencing of the plan. It gives us an opportunity to refine it. We let the virus spread. An antidote will be discovered, offered and applied. The virus will be stopped. Unfortunately, that same antidote will not be effective in the other areas of the world, once we implement infection."

Foxworth said, "Go on."

"Before the virus is contained the US government will be forced to quarantine parts of the country. Martial law will be necessary. The detention centers are empty and ready. It's an election year. Rice will be blamed. It might be an opportunity to remove him, one way or another."

Heads nodded. So far, they were with him.

"What is your exposure?"

"Minimal. There is no evidence of anything. I don't know how the Project found out about Demeter, but Lodge is working on that as we speak. The President cannot act openly without proof. All evidence regarding Demeter was destroyed in the attack on my facility. They cannot prove I have any involvement. Once I introduce the antidote no one would dare confront me."

Foxworth considered Dansinger's words. "Very well. We will take this under further discussion. Harold, you will keep us updated on your progress."

Under the words Dansinger heard a warning.

Dansinger's screen went blank.

CHAPTER FIFTY-ONE

Alexei Vysotsky listened to Korov's report.

"You are certain the virus was destroyed?"

"Yes. For the moment, Demeter is halted."

"For the moment."

"The laboratory and stockpiles are gone. But there must be other laboratories. I think we've bought time, not an end to the threat."

"What are the Americans doing?"

"We meet today to discuss the next steps. I believe they are genuine in their desire to smash this."

"Lodge?"

"That is one of the subjects of this meeting."

"They have accepted you?"

"They have. They are fearless, a very accomplished group. I wish I'd had them with me in Chechnya."

"High praise from you, Arkady."

"They earned it."

"Nonetheless, they are Americans. Do not forget that. Trust only goes so far."

"Of course, sir."

"Continue to observe and report."

Korov put away his phone. Vysotsky's comment annoyed him. He hadn't been in that compound. Carter and the others had earned his respect. More than that, they'd earned a measure of trust. Vysotsky would never understand that.

Different countries, different uniforms, same dedication. The same code. The code crossed all boundaries when men fought together.

His feelings confused him. He poured a cup of coffee and walked to the window. He'd always thought of America as the enemy. That hadn't changed. What confused him was his acceptance into this group, however temporary or expedient it might be. Korov knew the reverse would not be true. He couldn't even conceive of such a thing. It was bizarre. Even more bizarre, the Project wasn't a military unit like Zaslon. It was an intelligence group. Not exactly spies, in the traditional way. More like the sharp point of a rapier wielded to end threats before they'd fully begun.

He didn't understand Harker's actions. It wasn't the way things operated in his world. He slept in a hotel with free access to come and go, instead of a barracks somewhere under close surveillance. No one questioned him about carrying a weapon. He belonged to one of Russia's most secretive and effective units, yet he was allowed freedom in the heart of the American empire. It simply didn't compute.

Outside the hotel window the air was gray with smog, hazy, the sky overcast.

He thought about the woman, Connor. She was part of the combat team. Women were not assigned to operations like this in Russia. He didn't think they were here, either. She had done as well as the men. It surprised him. It hadn't escaped him that she and Carter were sleeping together. You could always tell. She was very attractive. In another time and place...he put that distracting thought aside.

Korov thought Carter as good a small force leader as he had ever seen. He'd accomplished the mission with cool efficiency against unfavorable odds.

In spite of himself, Korov found himself liking the Americans. They'd made him part of the team. The real test would come when he learned what they planned for their Director of Central Intelligence. In Russia, such a powerful man would be protected, invulnerable.

Arkady stared out the window at streams of cars crawling along a distant highway. He had no illusions about the political labyrinths inside the Kremlin. In Russia, it would be difficult to convince the leadership to make someone like Lodge disappear. More likely the accuser would be the one to disappear. What would Harker do?

That was another thing that confused him. A black ops intelligence unit run by a woman. He had to hand it to her, she didn't dance around what had to be done. She didn't seem concerned about possible repercussions from the attack.

All in all, this had turned into the most interesting assignment he'd ever had.

CHAPTER FIFTY-TWO

Stephanie was running late. She stepped out of the elevator in her parking garage and walked toward her car. Her shoes sounded loud in the echoing space. If Beltway traffic wasn't bad she might make it on time. Yeah, right, she thought. That's on the order of Moses parting the Red Sea.

She reached her car, a sensible Toyota Avalon. Enough luxury and power without getting into the really high end stuff. It was a lovely blue color. She liked her car. She pushed the remote and heard the beep as the doors unlocked. She opened the door. She heard a sound like a hissing snake and felt a sudden sharp pain and looked down at a dart sticking in her leg. She felt dizzy. The keys fell from her hand.

She woke lying on a cot. A small window well high up on the wall let in enough light to see a square room of unfinished concrete. A camera watched from the ceiling. The door was made of gray steel. A metal toilet without a seat took up one corner. The only other features were a water tap in the wall and a drain in the center of the floor.

A shot of fear cleared the fog from her mind. She sat up, awkwardly. Her right arm jerked back. Handcuffs shackled her to the cot. The cot was bolted to the floor.

The last thing...yes, opening the car door. Something in her leg. A tranquilizer dart.

She was in a cell. Not thinking, she felt for her gun. The empty holster mocked her. The handcuffs rattled.

Except for a headache and a queasy feeling in her stomach, she was unharmed. Her skirt was smudged with something, maybe from the garage floor. She had a scrape on her leg.

They'd taken her watch. Stephanie had no idea how long she'd been unconscious. She guessed a few hours. She took a deep breath, calming herself. Suddenly she was angry. She raised her free arm and gave the camera her middle finger. Maybe that would get someone's attention.

CHAPTER FIFTY-THREE

Harker sighed. Ronnie had shiny new crutches and a cast on his right leg. Lamont's arm was back in a sling. Nick came in walking like he had a board strapped on his back.

"Maybe we should just set up an ER in the hall. Has anyone seen Stephanie?"

"No." Headshakes.

"We'll start without her. Good work in Texas. We've stopped them, for now." She looked at the picture on her desk of the Twin Towers. She picked up the silver pen. "What shall we do about Lodge?"

"Maybe Rice can handle it." Nick's back ached like hell. It was black and blue and red, a bad sunset from a grade B movie.

"Nothing's changed. We've got no proof of anything."

"We could put pressure on Dansinger," Lamont said. "If he gives Lodge up, he could get a deal from Rice."

"For someone who was about to kill millions of people? I don't think so."

"Dansinger might not know that."

"We could, how do you say, 'grab' him. Dansinger, not Lodge. Or maybe Lodge himself?" Korov watched Harker.

"Lodge is too risky. Maybe later, but not now. Rice can only protect us so far."

"We could bug him," Ronnie said.

"Any bug we got in place wouldn't last long. Everywhere he goes is swept three or four times a day."

"Steph could help," Nick said. "She's hanging out with Lucas and Lucas works for Hood. Maybe he can find something out."

"What if Hood is part of this?" Harker said.

"He doesn't strike me as someone who'd get in bed with Lodge. He doesn't like Lodge, he's ambitious, he wants Lodge's job. That might work to our advantage."

"If you're wrong it will tip our hand."

"What hand? If I were Lodge, I'd have figured out who was behind Texas. I'll bet a year's pay he knows it was us."

Everyone thought about that. Nick's ear began itching. He tugged on it.

Selena pushed hair away. "Lodge won't take it lying down. He's got to move against us, do something."

"I know what I would do." They turned to Korov. "I would seek information. I would not ask nicely."

"How would you get it?" Harker asked.

"From one of us."

CHAPTER FIFTY-FOUR

Bright lights came on. Two large men brought a chair into the cell. Stephanie watched them. The chair was made of heavy wood. The seat was cut out in the middle, like a child's potty training chair. This chair was full size, with leather straps fixed to the arms and legs. Stephanie tried to hold down her fear. A third man entered, carrying an aluminum case. He reminded her of a bank clerk from a black and white movie about the Depression. He was short and balding and small, prissy looking, with a prim brown mustache and a pinched chin. He wore a vest and round, steel rimmed glasses. His lips were pursed. He eyed her with indifference. It chilled her.

"Strip her. Put her in the chair."

The men came over to her. One of them wrapped his huge arms around her while the other unshackled her from the cot. She struggled and tried to bite him.

He punched her in the stomach. She doubled over. They ripped off her clothes and tossed them aside. They carried her squirming to the chair while the prissy man watched and smoked a cigarette. They sat her in the chair and tied her down with the leather straps and left the room. A minute later they came back carrying a table and a box. They set the table down by the chair with the box on top of it.

"That's all." The third man dismissed them. "Close the door behind you."

"Yes, sir." They left the room. The door clanged shut. She was alone with the prim man.

He smiled, an unpleasant smile. "In this room we are going to get to know each other."

"Fuck you."

"No, not that. Something much more...intimate."

He hummed to himself and laid the aluminum case on the table. He opened it. The lid contained a row of rubber topped vials, three syringes, swabs, alcohol and something in a tube.

From the bottom of the case he took out a white cloth bundle. He unrolled it and placed it on the table. It contained a polished scalpel, a narrow forceps of surgical steel, a set of three different kinds of pliers and an assortment of odd shaped pointed probes.

He opened the box. It had a large car battery, wire leads and a smaller box with a dial.

Steph's breath came faster. It was just a battery. How much pain could he inflict with a battery? She could handle it. She told herself she could handle it. What did he want? Who was he?

"Let me explain why you are here. I advise you to speak civilly to me. Understand?" His voice was quiet.

Her lips were dry. "Yes."

"You are going to tell me about Demeter. How did you know about it?"

"I don't know what you're talking about."

"Yes, they always say that. Of course you know what I am talking about. Please do not waste our time together. You are Stephanie Willits. You work for a covert unit called the Project. You found out about Demeter. I want to know how."

Steph was silent.

"Cat got your tongue? No matter."

The man seemed to be coming alive as he spoke. A light sheen of sweat covered his forehead. His eyes darted over her naked body. He took a syringe from the case, selected a vial of clear liquid, filled the syringe, squirted a bit into the air. Her upper and lower arms were clamped tight to the chair. He probed for a vein, swabbed the spot with alcohol and injected her. In a few seconds she felt a rush of heat over her body. Her pupils dilated. The room was suddenly too bright. She felt something else.

Sexual arousal.

"Interesting, isn't it?" he said. "The effect lasts about an hour. Our Chinese friends developed this as an aphrodisiac.

Of course, they use a much smaller amount. It has other applications with a dose like yours. Let me show you."

He leaned close. She could smell his foul breath. He extended his forefinger and ran a yellowed nail lightly over her breast. The sensation was like nothing she'd ever experienced. Every nerve ending was incredibly alive. The feel of the nail across her skin was almost unbearable, intense, just short of pain, on the border between pain and ecstasy. She gasped. She couldn't help herself. She jerked away against the restraining straps. They felt like barbed wire

"That was just my finger." He picked up the scalpel. The edge gleamed. He held it up in front of her eyes. He moved it back and forth. Her eyes followed the shining blade. He smiled.

"Tell me how you found out about Demeter."

Steph tried to control her fear. "I don't know anything about Demeter. I don't know what you're talking about. I'm just a secretary."

"Oh, very good. I can see you will be entertaining."

He took the dull handle end of the scalpel and pushed it against her arm. The pain was intense, as if someone had stabbed her. She screamed and tried to pull away. The straps around her arms and legs were like bands of fire.

He set the scalpel down, reached over to the box and took out two wire leads with large metal alligator clips on the end. He turned the dial.

"Watch." He brought the clips close. A blue-white electric arc sparked between them. He took the clips and briefly touched them to her, one on each leg.

The pain was total, instant, overwhelming. Her bladder let go. When she opened her eyes he was watching her. He lit another cigarette.

"That was at the lowest voltage. The battery is only twelve volts. It won't kill you. The next time I use this I will clip one lead to your nipple. Guess where the other one goes?" He giggled. "Can you imagine what that will feel like?"

He took a deep drag on the cigarette and blew smoke at the ceiling.

"There is an interesting effect I haven't shared with you. As your body is overloaded with sensation, it will begin to shut down the response. That is when I increase the voltage."

"Fuck you, you creepy prick."

"Will you tell me what I want to know?"

She shook her head. He sighed, the sound of a disappointed parent.

"Why don't you think about it for a bit?" He glanced at his watch. "I am going to come back in exactly two hours. I will inject a new dose. Then you will tell me everything."

He put out the cigarette on her naked thigh. By the time she stopped screaming he had left the room.

CHAPTER FIFTY-FIVE

They hadn't come up with anything. Harker wondered out loud where Stephanie had got to when her phone rang. She listened for a moment. She tensed. She put the phone down.

"Someone's grabbed Steph. They found her keys and her purse by her car. In the garage of her building."

"Lodge." Nick's ear itched. "It has to be Lodge."

She nodded. "If Lodge took her, she's in one of his safe houses. We need to find it."

"How?"

Elizabeth clasped her hands together. "Hood would know where they all are."

"But will he tell us?"

"You know him, ask him. Call him now. Lodge will do anything to find out what Steph knows. Do I need to paint a picture?"

"Don't call Hood." It was Selena. "Call Lucas. Steph says he's in love with her."

Harker raised her eyebrows.

Selena said, "Lucas has a personal investment, Hood doesn't. He doesn't know Stephanie or have any reason to care about her. Lucas might know where the safe house is, or get Hood to cooperate."

He punched in Lucas' number. Monroe picked up on the second ring.

"Monroe."

"Lucas, Nick Carter."

"Hey, Nick, to what do I owe the pleasure?"

"We on a secure line?"

"I'll call you back." He hung up.

Nick waited. The phone rang.

"What's up?"

"Lucas, Steph's in trouble. Someone grabbed her."

Nick heard Monroe suck in his breath. "What do you mean, someone grabbed her?"

"In her parking garage. Her keys and purse were found by her car. We think it was Lodge."

"Lodge? Why?"

"It's complicated. I need you to trust me and I need your help."

"What do you need?"

"We think Lodge took her somewhere to interrogate her. He'd have to get rough to get anything. We need the location of CIA safe houses in the immediate area."

"Are you saying she's going to be tortured? That Lodge is behind it?"

"That's what we think."

"Christ, Nick."

"Yeah."

"Those locations are classified."

"Yeah, that's why I called you."

"You couldn't get in without ID."

"You can come with us."

"Christ, Nick, let me think for a minute."

Carter waited.

"There are three possibilities. Two are in D.C., an apartment and a town house. There are neighbors. There's a house and grounds by itself near Alexandria. If I wanted to interrogate someone, that's where I'd take them. We've used it in the past."

"Where is it?"

"Give me fifteen minutes. Meet me in your parking lot. I'll pick you up." Lucas hung up.

"He's on his way." Nick repeated what Lucas had told him.

Harker picked up her pen. "Nick. You, Korov and Selena." She paused. "This could go bad. Try not to kill anyone. I don't think Lodge will be there, but if he is, for God's sake don't shoot him."

"If he hurt Steph, you might want to tell that to Lucas," Nick said.

CHAPTER FIFTY-SIX

Nick ran it down for Lucas on the drive. When he told him about Korov, Lucas gave the Russian a hard look in the mirror. As he talked about Lodge, Monroe's face tightened.

Lucas Monroe had made it from the mean streets of Washington to the sixth floor at Langley. He was one of the most successful field agents in CIA history. For a black man in a culture rooted in the old WASP Ivy League, it was a hell of an achievement. He'd earned it, every hard step of the way.

"That bastard. You should have told us before. Hood could have helped." His tone was accusing.

"I couldn't, Lucas. We didn't know if Hood was part of it. We couldn't be sure. Stephanie couldn't tell you. You know how it is."

"Yeah. Need to know." He focused on the road. "If Lodge has hurt her..." He didn't finish.

The safe house was a two story colonial set behind a high brick wall. A heavy steel gate blocked the entrance to a blacktop drive. A small guard shack stood outside the gate. A man wearing a sport jacket and sunglasses came out of the shack as they pulled up. He didn't wear a tie and his shirt was open at the collar. There was a bulge under his jacket.

"Can I help you," he said.

Lucas showed his ID. With Alpha clearance he had access to any CIA facility anywhere in the world.

"Sir, I don't have you on my list. I need to call it in."

"Do you recognize my clearance?"

"Yes, sir."

"Then you know I don't need to be on your list. Open the gate."

"Sir, Director Lodge..."

"You like guard duty?"

"It's okay, sir."

"Open the damned gate, or you're going to be doing it in Afghanistan."

"I'm sorry, sir. I have orders from the DCI himself. I need to call it in."

The movement was casual. Korov opened the rear door and got out of the car. He stretched.

"Beautiful day," he said.

He moved so fast Nick barely saw it happen. Korov drove stiffened fingers into the man's solar plexus and slammed his elbow into the side of his head. The guard collapsed. Korov dragged him into the shack. He pressed a switch. The gate slid open. Korov ripped wires from the wall. He came out of the shack and got back in the car.

"What was that?"

"Feeds to the cameras." Korov nodded at a camera by the gate. "Perhaps they know we are coming, perhaps not."

"You kill him?"

"No."

Lucas shook his head. "I hope you're right about this."

They drove up to the entrance and got out of the car.

Lucas took out his pistol. "I know the house. There's a foyer and then a long hall down the middle. Front to back, you pass a living room, dining room and kitchen on the right. Music room, library, den on the left. Doors to each opening on the hall. Four bedrooms upstairs. The interrogation rooms are in the basement. If they have her, that's where she'll be. The entrance is past the kitchen, on the right. One flight of steps."

They drew their weapons. Lucas went in front. Carter, Selena and Korov stood to the side. Lucas pulled open the front door, using it as a partial shield. Nothing happened. They entered the house and fanned out across the foyer. Korov left the door open behind them.

Nick signaled with his hand, pointing fingers. Korov, Selena to the left. Lucas and himself to the right.

Selena was about to enter the music room when a man came out.

"Who..."

Selena moved in a blur, three strikes, the last to the base of the skull. The man fell unconscious to the floor. Korov followed her in. They cleared the music room and entered the library. The room was a window into past centuries, floor to ceiling shelves filled with hundreds of volumes. A large world globe rested in a cradle on a polished mahogany table. Prints of English country scenes hung on the walls. A sliding ladder ran on tracks along the shelves. Sunlight streamed through French doors opening onto a patio and garden. An oriental rug covered the floor. The room would have pleased Ben Franklin or Thomas Jefferson.

A man came into the room from the den. He saw them, pulled a gun and fired at Selena. Korov shot him, the sound an unexpected offense in that elegant room. Footsteps pounded on the ceiling above.

A second man came out of the den firing. Something plucked at her sleeve. She dove to the side. Korov went the other way. She rolled to her feet and brought her Glock dead center on the man's chest and squeezed off three quick rounds. The shots drove him backward into the table with the globe, sending it tumbling across the rug. She got up and ran to the den. It was empty. She went back into the library.

Korov went to the door of the library and ducked back as bullets splintered the enameled frame over his head. Selena heard Nick's heavy .45. She heard shots from upstairs. Two, maybe three shooters.

She pictured the house, the stairs, the hall. She was directly across from the open dining room door. She dropped low, breathed and somersaulted across the hall, firing at a shape on the stairs. A body tumbled down the wooden steps. She rolled into the dining room and ended up at Nick's feet.

"Nice move. Where'd you learn that one?"

"Aikido." She reached around the corner, fired blind up the staircase. "How many?"

"Three. You got one, I think."

A sudden tearing sound ripped the air, followed by a yell and heavy thumping as another body rolled down the stairs.

"What was that?" Lucas said.

"Our Russian buddy. He's got a neat toy."

They heard the tearing sound again, then silence. The acrid scent of the guns was strong in the air.

Korov walked into the dining room. "Safe, I think."

"Still the basement."

They stepped into the hall. Blood trailed down the steps in thin red waterfalls from two bodies sprawled on the stairs. A third was draped over a balcony railing on the second floor. The top of his head was missing. Blood dripped in a steady stream from the wound, splashing on the parquet floor below.

"They were kind of determined," Lucas said.

"Something's not right." He looked at one of the bodies. "I recognize this guy. He was kicked out of the Agency two years ago."

"Someone came out of the den shooting," Selena said. "We didn't have a choice."

"Don't worry about it." Nick moved to the door leading to the basement. He put his hand on the knob.

"Ready?"

CHAPTER FIFTY-SEVEN

Bob Elroy stood in the bed of a red Ford pickup, looking out over his wasted fields. Two other men stood next to him. Jack Wemberly was the local Farm Bureau man and USDA's man on the spot. He and Bob went back a long ways. Wemberly wore Levis and a light yellow checked shirt open at the collar. His sandy hair was covered by a brown Bailey felt hat, well worn, the brim curled like a Stetson.

The second man was as out of place as an elephant in a pigsty, or so Bob told Mae later over supper. The second man had introduced himself as Agent Brown. He didn't say what agency and Bob didn't ask. What difference did it make? Brown wore a black suit, a white shirt and a dark tie. His sunglasses were smoky, almost black. His shoes were shiny black, or had been, before he'd trudged through the fields with Elroy and Wemberly. Now the shine was covered with dust and debris. The debris came from dead, black plants stretching away as far as any of the men could see.

Men in white hazmat suits walked through the field taking samples. Government experts. As if hazmat suits made a damn bit of difference.

"This is awful." Wemberly shook his head.

"Yep." Bob couldn't take his eyes away from the blight. "It's gone way past my property. Showing up miles away from here. Everywhere the wind blows, seems to me."

"And everything is dead?"

"Everything that grows, anyway. Doesn't seem to bother the animals. Doesn't do anything to the feed corn we got stockpiled, or the hay. Just the live crops." His voice was bitter. "I'm finished. All of us around here are."

"Those are experts, Bob. They'll figure this out."

"They will? That going to put food on the table, Jack? Pay my loans?"

"I'll talk to the bank. The government will help."

Bob snorted. "Sure it will. Whyn't you have a nice talk with Agent Brown, here. He's from the government. I gotta feed the pigs."

He jumped down from the truck and stalked toward the barn. Brown watched him go.

"What's his politics?"

Wemberly stared at him. "His politics? What the hell has that got to do with anything? Bob's a farmer, for Christ's sake. He votes for the land."

"This started on his land."

"You think he did this on purpose? Poisoned his land?"

"Maybe not, but someone did. His land and a hundred and thirty thousand acres."

"What?" Jack tried to comprehend the figure. He couldn't get his mind around it.

"A hundred and thirty thousand and spreading. It'll be public by tomorrow. No harm in telling you now."

"You think this is some kind of terrorist thing? Who did you say you worked for?"

"I didn't say. And yes, it could be a terrorist attack. Bio war. Maybe the beginning of something bigger."

"Agent Brown," Jack said, "if that's really your name. Look at that." He swept his arm out at the blackened fields. "It doesn't get bigger than that."

CHAPTER FIFTY-EIGHT

The steps going down into the basement were part of the old house. At the bottom everything turned to new concrete. A lighted corridor ten feet wide and ten feet high ran the length of the house above. The stairs came out by a furnace and utility room set at one end. At the other end of the corridor were two metal doors with view plates. The doors were closed. The view plates were closed. It was cool in the basement.

They moved silent as cats down the corridor and paused. Nick listened. He heard nothing. He signaled. Right door first. He opened it onto an empty room. He took in the cot, the toilet, the camera on the ceiling.

He shook his head at the others. One room left. What if she wasn't in there?

He gestured for the others to stand out of sight and opened the door, pistol ready. He saw Stephanie.

She was strapped naked into a chair. Her eyes were wide. An odd little man stood behind her, holding a syringe filled with a dark fluid next to her throat in one hand. The point of the needle was next to her jugular. Nick could see the vein throbbing. He could smell Stephanie's fear. There was a puddle of liquid under her chair. In his other hand the man held a 9mm pistol aimed at Nick's chest.

"Stop."

Nick froze where he was.

"Put down your weapon."

"Not yet. Who are you?"

"This syringe is filled with an especially nasty poison. There is no antidote. She will die in terrible pain. It takes several minutes. Put down your weapon. I will not ask again."

He leaned close to Stephanie. "Tell him I mean what I say."

"He means it, Nick. He does."

"Okay. I'm putting it down." Nick bent and put the .45 on the floor. He straightened.

"Kick the gun over here. Easy."

The gun rasped across the floor and stopped a foot from the chair.

"What do you want?"

"This is not a discussion. Raise your hands. Move to the side." The little man gestured with his head. He kept the gun pointed at Nick's chest. "That way."

Nick raised his hands and stepped to the side.

"Now tell the others to come inside and put their weapons on the floor."

"Others?"

"Don't play games. I've got nothing to lose. She does. You do. Tell them to come in, one by one. Weapons on the floor and kick them toward me or she dies."

"Korov," Nick called out. "He's got her strapped to a chair and a needle at her neck. He'll kill her. Come in and do as he says."

The man sighed. "The woman too. I know she's there, Carter. Quick."

Knows my name.

Korov came in and then Selena. They put their guns on the floor, kicked them toward the chair and moved over to Nick. In the hall, Lucas waited unseen. He thought about Stephanie. He felt the cool anger descend, the killer angel.

"Now lie down, except the woman."

They lay down. Selena stood waiting, hands raised.

"You. Get on your hands and knees and crawl to the front of the chair."

Selena got down on the floor. The surface was rough against her skin. She focused on Stephanie's eyes as she crawled to the chair, trying to send a message. A subtle change came into Steph's face.

Selena reached the chair.

"Unbuckle the leg straps. If you do anything else, if this one moves, she dies."

Steph sat rigid in the chair. Selena undid the straps, one by one. "Now the arms. Right one first. Be very careful."

Selena unbuckled the straps. Stephanie sat still.

"Very good. Now back away and lie down with the others."

"You can't kill us all."

He laughed. "I can certainly kill your friend here. You too. Back away and lie down."

Selena crawled backwards and lay down on the floor.

"Stand up," he said to Stephanie. "Be careful. The needle could slip."

He moved behind her as she stood, keeping his pistol trained on the others. They watched from the floor. His left arm pressed against her, keeping her tight against him. Through his pants she felt his erection against her naked buttocks.

His breath was hot in her ear. "We're going to back out the door and lock your friends inside. Be careful. We'll continue our session somewhere else. It's gotten crowded in here, don't you think?"

In the hall, Lucas waited. One chance.

As they backed into the hall Lucas pulled the hand with the needle away from Stephanie's neck and twisted the gun away. Stephanie broke free. Lucas kept his grip on the man's hand and drove the needle down, deep into the side of her captor's leg. He felt the needle strike bone. He pushed the plunger in all the way.

The man screamed and fell to the floor. The others came out of the cell. Selena went to Stephanie. Nick handed Selena his jacket. She draped it around Stephanie's body and put her arms around her.

"It's okay, Steph. You're all right now. You're safe."

Steph began sobbing on Selena's shoulder.

On the floor, the little man writhed and shrieked. Froth and spittle foamed from his mouth. His eyes were wide, terrified. His body went into terrible spasms on the floor. He became rigid, then arched backward in an impossible curve. Nick heard bones snapping. He gave a final scream of unbearable agony and died.

Lucas looked down at the body.
"Asshole," he said.
Then he went to Stephanie and held her close.

CHAPTER FIFTY-NINE

Lucas and Stephanie lay on her bed, face to face in each other's arms. He felt her warm breath on his shoulder, the pulse of her life beating against him. Lucas stroked her hair. It was damp from the long shower she'd taken when they'd gotten to her apartment. She hadn't talked since they'd left the safe house. It was beginning to worry him. He held her and tried to surround her with calm, with safety.

Lucas knew what it was like to be tortured. He still bore the scars. The anticipation was almost as bad as the actual act. Knowing you were helpless. Knowing you were at the mercy of a psychopath.

Lucas was no choir boy. He'd grown up in the ghetto. He'd been an agent for a long time. He'd done and seen his share of things no one should have to endure in the name of duty or expediency or survival. But he had never resorted to inflicting excruciating pain to gain intelligence. Torture disgusted him. He thought of Wendell Lodge and what had happened to Stephanie and for the first time felt the kind of hatred that would inflict pain for its own sake. He imagined Lodge helpless before him. Maybe strapped naked on a hard chair, in a cold room where knives gleamed under harsh light.

Steph stirred.

"I didn't tell him. But I would have. Whatever he wanted."

"Sshh. I know. You did good. It's all right now."

"His eyes. He had awful eyes. He liked what he was doing."

"They always do. But he won't hurt you or anyone else again."

"How did you find me?"

"Nick called me. They found your purse in the garage, they knew you'd been taken. It had to be Lodge, they said. That house was the best bet."

"What if you'd been wrong?"

"I wasn't, that's what matters."

"The drug he gave me. It was awful. He told me it would wear off and I should think about it. He told me he was coming back."

"Yeah, they like to do that, people like him."

"He was getting ready to start again when the shooting began upstairs. That's when he put that poison in the syringe. He told me what it would do. In detail." She shuddered. "Then he just waited for you to find us."

Lucas stoked her hair.

"I love you."

"I love you, too, Steph."

"What are you going to do about Lodge?"

"I don't know."

CHAPTER SIXTY

James Rice thought there were times when being President was the worst job anyone could imagine. Like now. He sat alone in the Oval Office, at the power center of the world. Outside the White House the city got ready for another evening. The folder on his desk contained the reports on Nebraska. The analysis was grim. The damage was spreading at an alarming pace, a vast, diseased sore oozing in the heart of America.

Two hours earlier he'd had a meeting with the experts and the Joint Chiefs and the Secretary of Agriculture. The Pentagon thought it could be a terrorist attack. The Generals were arguing about what to do, how to respond. The stress level within the administration and the Pentagon was rising. Rice had boosted the alert status to DEFCON3. He hadn't revealed Lodge's involvement. It was a hell of a mess.

Harker had briefed him about Texas. She would take care of Dansinger. Rice had to take care of the country. The experts agreed that only one solution was available.

Fire.

The crop virus was airborne and as yet, unstoppable. He had to do something and he had to do it soon. Rice let out a long breath. His actions were going to cost him the election. But this went beyond politics. It was why Truman had that famous sign on his desk about where the buck stopped. Decisive action was needed now.

He'd thought about calling in the Speaker and the Majority Leader and decided against it. They'd balk. If Congress got involved, if he allowed politics to dictate action, the delay would doom America's crops. It could not be allowed to happen. It was his job to make sure it didn't happen, whatever the personal cost.

Rice picked up his phone.

"Get me the Governor of Nebraska."

"Yes, Mr. President."

While he waited, Rice thought about his days in Vietnam. They were bad memories. He was about to bring back a terrible echo of that horrific war. At least this time around it was to assure life, not destruction. Governor Rowena Wheeling came on the line.

"Mr. President."

"Governor, thank you for taking my call. I'm calling about the crop blight."

Rice knew what he was going to do and he knew Governor Wheeling was not going to like it. The fact that she belonged to the opposition party didn't make things any easier. Rice was about to assert the enormous power of the government in dramatic and public fashion. There were going to be problems on every level.

"Mr. President." Her voice was neutral. "I'm told by my advisors this thing cannot be stopped. I hope you are calling to tell me something different."

"Actually, Governor, there is a way. But it will create severe disruption in your state. I am going to need your cooperation. I hope you will be willing to give it."

"Sir, I will of course do anything I can." Her voice was wary. What was up?

"There's no way to sugar coat this, Rowena." Rice hoped the use of her name would add a personal touch. It was his style. "I'm declaring an emergency in Nebraska. I want you to initiate mandatory evacuation procedures of the entire affected area and a radius of twenty miles around it. Beginning immediately. Use the National Guard to enforce it. I'm sending in additional military units to assist."

Stunned silence.

"Sir, you're talking about thousands of people."

"I know that, Governor. If people don't have somewhere to go the FEMA emergency shelters can handle them. Rail and truck transport will be provided. I'm hoping it won't be necessary, but I will declare martial law if needed. This has to be done now."

"What are you planning, sir? There will be problems."

Rice paused. He knew Wheeling was a rarity in the Governors' mansions, a centrist. Opposition party, yes. But a woman who sometimes backed his agenda, and as a result was often under siege from her own party. When she fought, she was fair. He decided to tell her more.

"Rowena, I'm going to tell you something. It's important you share this with no one. It's a question of national security." The magic words. "Can I trust you?"

"National security? Of course, sir."

"This must be kept quiet. We have uncovered a domestic plot to sabotage the crops."

He heard her gasp.

"This thing is man made? A terror plot?"

"Yes." Rice didn't think she needed to know that it had originally been aimed at Russia.

"We are working to discover a counter agent but it is uncertain it can be developed in time to prevent very large areas of contamination. In the event it cannot be obtained, I'm going to burn the entire area."

"Mr. President? Are you saying you want to burn up my state?"

"Just the infected areas. Fire is all we've got at this point to stop it. The weather is calm for the next two days. High winds are forecast after that. If this thing gets past your borders, we will lose tens of millions of acres of farmland and crops. I cannot allow that. I will ensure government assistance for the displaced."

"Like Katrina?" She was angry. "We all know how well that worked out."

"We've learned a lot since then." Rice allowed a hard edge to appear in his voice. "Governor, this is not an option. Your cooperation will be appreciated."

"Sir, two days isn't enough time."

"It has to be, Governor."

"Mr. President. You give me no choice. I will do as you say. But if you burn, I believe you will seal your defeat in the upcoming election."

"That is a risk I must take."
"Very well, sir. May God help you."
"May God help all of us, Governor."
 She hung up.

CHAPTER SIXTY-ONE

Harker's office felt oppressive. No one smiled. Stephanie was at home. The others were there, along with Lucas.

"Things are getting out of hand," Elizabeth said. "Rice has declared an emergency and is evacuating thousands of people in Nebraska. He's had to institute martial law. There's looting in the evacuated areas. The FEMA centers are getting crowded."

"What's he going to do?" Nick tugged on his ear.

"He intends to burn everything that's been affected."

"Burn it? The farms, everything?"

"Everything. It will cost him the election."

"How's he going to do it?" Lamont asked.

"Napalm."

"I thought all of it had been destroyed."

"Not quite. It seems we kept some back, just in case."

"Jesus. They never learn." Nick shook his head.

"It's called Operation Cleaner. The Air Force begins bombing tomorrow. They're coordinating with the various fire departments. Rice intends to go beyond the affected area in an effort to keep it from spreading any further. The media and the opposition are having a field day."

"What if it doesn't work?"

"Then the country is in big trouble. But there may be a way out. Dansinger must have figured out how to stop it once he got what he wanted. I've talked with Rice. Special Forces units should be hitting Dansinger's Utah research facility right about now. If there's an antidote it's probably there."

"So there might be time to stop this without burning everything up."

"If it exists and if it's there. If it's up and running before the bombers lift off."

"Where's Dansinger now?"

"Here in Washington to present his case for genetically engineered crops at a USDA conference. He just came back from Utah. Rice is giving us a free hand with him." She paused, thinking. "Lucas, is there anything Langley knows that would help?"

"I'm not sure what I can say. No offense, Korov. I appreciate what you did at the house."

"None is taken."

Harker picked up her pen. "Major Korov has a personal investment in our success for the sake of his nation. That's why he's here. No one's asking you to reveal classified information. If you know something, now's the time."

Nick watched Lucas struggle with something. "I can say this much. Hood is worried. Something a lot bigger than Lodge or Dansinger is going on. We're not sure what it is. We think Demeter may be part of it. Hood suspects a conspiracy that goes beyond our borders."

"An international conspiracy? To what end?"

"We don't know. Money, power, dominance, any or all of those things. That would fit with a desire to attack Russia. Any organization that would unleash something like Demeter has got to be uncovered and stopped. We have no real leads."

"I have an idea," Nick said. "Why don't we ask Dansinger about it?"

"Grab him?" Selena said.

"Turn about is fair play."

Korov was puzzled. "An idiom? Turn about?"

"They grabbed Steph. We return the favor."

CHAPTER SIXTY-TWO

Harold Dansinger looked at the papers displayed in the hotel lobby and smiled. Every paper carried a variation of the same story.

Nebraska In Flames
Thousands Evacuated

Air force bombers today began carpeting the farmlands of Nebraska with napalm in an effort to halt the spread of a destructive virus threatening America's crops. At an extraordinary press conference this morning, Press Secretary Ryan Atkinson announced that President Rice had ordered the destruction by fire of the infected areas.

"I just can't believe it," said Mary-Anne Carson, whose family has been farming for four generations in America's heartland. "They're going to burn everything. Our home, the barns, the crops, everything. Why is the President doing this to us? There must be a better way."

Critics called Rice's decision a blatant misuse of Presidential power without political or historical precedent...

One popular daily featured full color aerial shots of homes and cropland in flames. There were pictures of confused and angry people herded together at the FEMA shelters. Armed soldiers kept a watchful eye on the crowds. Martial law was in effect for the entire state.

Rice is finished, Dansinger thought.

He stepped from the entrance to his hotel and adjusted his famous Stetson. It was early evening in Washington, still light. He was mildly annoyed. His car wasn't here yet and for some reason he hadn't been able to reach Utah.

While he waited he thought about Nebraska. He planned to let the virus spread for a few more days. Then he would announce the discovery of an airborne antidote. He still didn't know how the virus had gotten loose, but it didn't matter. He'd be seen as a savior by the American people.

By then at least a million acres or more of prime American farmland would be a blackened waste. Studying the spread of the virus on a larger scale would allow him to refine the attack on Russia. That was a bonus. Also there would be profit opportunities for his genetic crops right here at home. So, perhaps it wasn't all bad.

The front of the hotel was graced by a high, sweeping portico. His car would be here at any moment. The afternoon was pleasant. Dansinger stepped toward the curb, looking for his driver. He saw two men coming toward him. Both had a military look. They were about the same size. One was blond, the other dark haired. Both wore suits. Both were armed, he could see the bulges under their jackets. The blond man seemed vaguely foreign.

"Harold Dansinger. Stop where you are." One of the men held up a credential holder with a picture and a gold badge.

Where was his car? He turned to look for it. There was a distant sound like a dull pop and that was when the bullet took him. The white Stetson turned red. His skull exploded like a melon. He slammed backward onto the pavement. People began screaming.

"Sniper," Nick yelled to Korov. They ducked behind a fat, round pillar holding up the portico. Chaos erupted in front of the hotel

They both had their guns out. Korov risked a glance. No one shot at him. They waited. There were no more shots.

Nick holstered his pistol. "He's gone. He wasn't after us."

Dansinger lay on his back in a spreading pool of blood. His head was oddly flat against the pavement.

Nick looked at the blood stained white Stetson. "Wrong color. It should have been black."

"What?"

"Never mind. Guess someone didn't want him answering any questions."

"This is something I would expect in Chechnya. I thought Washington was different."

"I guess not."

CHAPTER SIXTY-THREE

Dansinger's murder didn't make it past the second page. The front page was devoted to the disaster in Nebraska. 200,000 acres of prime farmland and hundreds of buildings had gone up in flames before the antidote had been found and applied. It looked like the virus had been stopped.

Rice was attacked from all sides. Congress was united in expressing righteous indignation that Rice had not consulted them before acting. There were threats of impeachment. The left screamed about napalm. The right wailed about the expense to taxpayers. Op Ed pundits posed pseudo-profound questions about morality, ethics and the Constitution, while the environmentalists made grave predictions of damage from the spraying. Lawsuits against the government appeared like mushrooms after rain.

The media found it convenient for the moment to ignore the truth, that the blight had been stopped in its tracks before it could spread any further. Reason might eventually prevail, but Nick wasn't holding his breath. Rice was in for a rough ride.

Steph was back. She was quiet. No one was surprised.

Harker tapped her pen. "Rice is giving public strokes to Governor Wheeling and releasing federal funds to help the farmers that were hit. Congress doesn't dare block it. It would cost them their seats if they did. But he's in a fight for his life as far as the election goes."

"Politics stinks." Nick scratched his ear. "Now Dansinger's gone, that leaves Lodge."

Korov thought, *Now we will get to it.*

"It so happens that the President agrees with you."

"Who killed Dansinger?"

"That's the question, isn't it? Rice wants us to confront Lodge in person. He specifically wants you and I to do it. Perhaps Lodge knows who shot our friend of the farmers. I thought we'd bring Major Korov along in the spirit of international cooperation. So he can report to his boss."

"Rice still doesn't know about Arkady?" Nick and Korov had begun using their first names with each other.

"No. He doesn't need to."

"What do you have in mind?"

"I've spoken with Hood. I don't think he's any part of this. He's arranged a meeting with Lodge."

"Where?"

"We'll beard the lion in his den. At his home in Virginia. It's set for this evening."

Korov looked lost.

Harker continued. "Selena and Lamont outside for backup. Ronnie and Steph can mind the fort. Hood will be there."

If Korov looked lost before, now he was totally confused.

"These idioms."

Nick laughed. "Don't worry about it, Comrade. We're going to put an end to this, tonight."

CHAPTER SIXTY-FOUR

Selena and Lamont waited in the car. They watched Clarence Hood meet Nick, Harker and Korov at the door of Lodge's Virginia home. All four went inside.

Lamont watched the door close. "I don't like this,"

"No."

"Let's scout out the area."

They got out of the car. A few evening birds sang to each other in the twilight. The lawns around the house were newly mowed. The clean scent of fresh cut grass filled the air. It was still warm from the day. They walked around the flower beds to the side of the house and paused at the corner. French doors led from a large patio into a lighted study. They had a good view. Lodge sat in a red leather chair behind a desk. Hood and the others came into the room. Hood closed the study door behind him and took a seat on Lodge's left, facing the others.

Selena and Lamont wore earpieces that let them hear everything. Watch and listen, Harker had said. Don't intervene unless you absolutely have to. Everyone was armed. Selena knew she and Lamont were strictly a last resort. Their job was out here, not in that room.

Harker settled herself in her chair.

"You've gone too far this time, Wendell. The President is concerned."

"My, right to the point, Director." Lodge's voice was contemptuous. "The President owes me and I intend to collect the debt. I know far too much and it's an election year. He will not be making any sudden changes at Langley."

"Is that a blackmail threat? Against the President?"

"I assume you are recording this. No, it's not a threat. It's a guarantee. I will destroy him. If Rice has any desire to remain in office, he will not interfere."

"Wendell." It was Hood. "They know."

"What do they know?"

"About Demeter and Dansinger. About Wilkinson and Campbell and the others."

"I wonder who told them?"

Nick's ear began itching. Elizabeth answered. "We have a video of a meeting you held with Dansinger and Wilkinson. Your security procedures are getting sloppy, Wendell."

"Ah, that explains it. It must have been in Texas. Harold always thought he was smarter than he was."

"Why don't you tell us about the Pentagon?" she said.

"The Pentagon?" Korov looked at her.

Lodge was pleased. "You see, Major Korov. You just can't trust her. She didn't tell you about Operation Black Harvest, did she?"

Elizabeth sighed. "It's a war game scenario that predicts total crop failure in Russia, with subsequent invasion in the guise of assistance."

Korov was getting angry. "This was created by your Pentagon? All of this?"

"No, It wasn't. It's a war game, a scenario, nothing more. I'm sure you have similar scenarios in Moscow?"

Korov didn't answer.

"She's telling the truth, Major. It wasn't the Pentagon." Hood reached under his jacket and took out a 9mm pistol. He pointed it at Korov. "But you won't have a chance to tell anyone about it."

Lodge smiled. He took a gun from under his desk and pointed it at Nick. He was left handed.

Outside the house, Selena turned to Lamont.

"Hood. He's a traitor. What do we do?"

"Be ready to act. Let Harker give us the cue."

With his right hand Lodge pressed a button under his desk. Steel shutters dropped down over the French doors, the windows, the entrance to the study. The room was sealed.

"Shit," Lamont said.

"The front." They ran to the front of the house. The door was locked. All the windows were sealed. They could hear Lodge's voice over their earpieces.

"My own version of a panic room. But it's not me who should be panicked."

"You feeling panicked, Arkady?"

"No, Nick. Are you?"

"I know what you're thinking, Carter. Don't try it. You'll never get your weapons out in time. I suggest we talk this out before someone does something stupid."

Nick remembered the video. Something familiar about one of the people he couldn't see. He looked at Hood.

"You were at that meeting."

"Yes, I was."

"You've known about this all along."

Hood shrugged.

"You son of a bitch. We trusted you."

"It's wise to keep trust close, Nick."

Harker put her hand on Nick's arm. "Who killed Dansinger, Wendell?"

"I don't know. Whoever it was did us all a favor."

The look he gave her was one of pure hatred. "I've had enough of you, Harker, and your little group. Whoever you have outside will not be able to get in here."

Nick figured he could get one of them before they got him. He made ready.

Lodge said, "Clarence, I think it's time to end this, don't you?"

"I certainly do, Wendell."

Hood swung his pistol to the right and fired at close range. The bullet took Lodge in the temple and blew out the side of his head in a spray of blood and bone. He flew sideways in his chair. The body sprawled against the red leather. The gun dropped from his hand.

The others sat frozen. Hood ignored them. He stood, wiped down his pistol, placed it in Lodge's left hand and squeezed the hand around it. He took out a small plastic bag filled with black grains and blew some on Lodge's hand and sleeve, sprinkled some on his shirt.

"A shame the DCI saw no alternative but suicide when confronted with his exposure," Hood said.

The instant of paralysis had passed. All three had their guns out. Hood reached under the lip of the desk and pressed the panic button. The shutters rolled back into place. Outside, a bird sounded a pleasant trill in the calm Virginia evening.

Selena and Lamont burst into the room, guns leveled. Hood lifted his hands.

"Please don't shoot. Director, I think we need to continue this conversation elsewhere. And I believe Major Korov would like to talk with his superior."

CHAPTER SIXTY-FIVE

They'd driven back to the Project in silence. Now they were in Harker's office.

"I really need a bigger office. All right, Clarence. Out with it."

"I apologize for the deception, Director. It was necessary. Lodge was cautious. He had to be stopped permanently. I felt that you and Major Korov needed to be sure it was over."

"Did Rice put you up to this?"

"Oh, no. I would never involve him in something like this."

"Did you have Dansinger killed?"

"I did not. But I have my suspicions. I just can't prove any of it."

"We're listening."

"Lodge approached me soon after he made DCI. At first, nothing firm, just sounding me out. How did I feel about the growing threat Moscow posed? Did I think some proactive measures were needed to slow them down? Would I be able to determine the true course of Russia's intentions? Like that. At first it seemed like normal things, the kinds of things we do at Langley."

Korov remained silent, but his look spoke volumes.

"I always felt he was holding something back. It's my job, you know. To know when people are concealing something. I went along with him. I'm not a Russophobe, but I decided that would be a good way to gain his trust. So I became his echo whenever he began ranting."

"He ranted?"

"Frequently. Lodge was a fanatic. He hated Russia. Then he introduced me to Dansinger. Eventually they brought me into the plot."

"Why didn't you blow the whistle?" Elizabeth said.

Korov looked blank for a moment.

"Because it wasn't just Lodge and Dansinger. That is something we must pursue. I believe Dansinger was part of a larger organization and was following their agenda. I also believe they killed him because of your actions. When you attacked his compound and destroyed their stockpiles of the virus, you exposed him. I think they wanted to make sure he couldn't talk."

"You're saying you didn't go to the President because you wanted to expose a larger plot?"

"Exactly."

"Was Lodge part of this organization?"

"No. I'm sure he wasn't. But I know Dansinger promised him the White House in four years. He told him his friends could assure it."

Nick remembered what Adam had told him in the back of that armored Cadillac.

"Jesus," Lamont said. "Who has the power to do that?"

"Apparently someone who doesn't believe in democracy."

"Why Russia?"

"It's the key. If they had succeeded, it would have been the start of a financial and military empire. Think of the strategic position. The Middle East, China, Southeast Asia, Japan, all within easy reach in the future. The oil fields in the Ukraine. Secure power in Russia under a guise of assistance, then have troops in place, then make your move."

Korov shook his head. "It would never have worked. You do not understand Russia. We would never surrender."

"I know that, Major. Anyone with an ounce of common sense knows that. But there have been many in the past who thought otherwise. Napoleon. Hitler. No one ever seems to learn from history, when it comes to Russia. None the less, there would have been a long occupation. Good business for the war mongers and death merchants. With someone like Lodge in the White House anything could become possible."

"What did Lucas know?" It was Stephanie.

"Only that I was worried about an unknown organization, a potential threat. He knew I was worried about Lodge, but not why. I couldn't risk telling anyone. I'm sure Lodge was monitoring me closely."

Steph settled back in her chair. Relieved.

"Was the Pentagon involved?"

"I hope not, but I don't know. The Black Harvest scenario is part of the bio-warfare planning. I'm certain there's an equivalent Russian war game. The Chinese as well. Everyone sees crops and food supplies as a soft target. A starving nation can be defeated."

The room was silent for a moment.

Selena took a breath. "That's criminal."

"That's war planning. The days of polite warfare are over. If there's a next one it will be total."

"War is a criminal act."

"Yes, Major, it is. So why have you and some of the others in this room prepared so well for it?"

"To defend our nation. From aggressors like Dansinger and Lodge."

Hood nodded. "Exactly. War initiated may be a criminal act, but war in defense of one's nation is an act of patriotism and honor. Unfortunately, soldiers pay the price for their leaders' greed and bad judgement."

Elizabeth brought them back into focus. "We're getting off the track. What do you actually know about this organization? Dansinger's?"

"Not much. There are hints of something but you can't track them down. Financial lines that disappear when you follow them. Political decisions that seem justified but erode freedom everywhere. Economic policies that concentrate wealth in the hands of a few. Cover ups. Facilities that appear intended for one thing but may be for another. Increased surveillance in every city. Much of it is here in the US, but it seems to be international. I know it's powerful and influential. I know it means us and everyone else no good."

"You are suggesting something along the line of a New World Order conspiracy."

"That's as good a name for it as anything else. I think the Demeter plot was part of a larger plan."

"But you have no proof."

"No."

"If this group exists, I don't think they're going to be very happy with what's happened in the last few days."

"I think you can count on that, Director. We'd all better watch our step."

CHAPTER SIXTY-SIX

Nick, Korov, Lamont and Ronnie sat at a back table in The Point, a bar favored by Special Ops personnel, active and retired. The place was busy. A bottle of vodka sat on the table. Ronnie had a coke in front of him. The others had empty four ounce glasses. Korov poured them full.

"In Russia, this is how we do it." He held up his full glass. "*Na Z'drovnya*. To your health." He downed the glass in a single gulp, waited to see if they would follow. Lamont and Nick held their glasses up. Ronnie lifted his coke. He never drank alcohol.

"*Na Z'drovnya*. Down the hatch." They drank. Korov filled the glasses again.

"Down the hatch?"

"Another idiom. We have lots of them."

"So do we."

They sipped.

"I return to Moscow tomorrow."

"What did your boss say, when you told him what happened?"

"He was impressed. As am I. We did not believe you would actually remove your CIA Director. The solution was elegant. He is pleased that the plot has been stopped."

"What do his bosses know?"

"That General Vysotsky has acted brilliantly to foil a threat against the Rodina. That the American CIA is in disarray. That one of his agents has successfully engaged with a secretive American intelligence unit and gained their trust."

"That would be you?"

Korov placed his hand over his heart and made a slight bow. He drained his glass. Nick filled it, then his own.

"Yeah, you'll probably get a medal," Lamont said.

"Maybe I have Vysotsky send you one."

They laughed. The bar was filling with men. Most of them had the look.

"This is a good place. If you come to Moscow I will show you a place like this."

"We might not be welcome."

"With me, you will be welcome." He made rings on the table with his wet glass.

"Nick. I hope we are never on, how you say, the opposite side."

"Maybe this will open a crack in the door. Our nations should not be enemies."

"But it is the way of things, is it not? When both countries want the same thing, there is trouble."

"Not if that thing is to our mutual benefit. Like what we did here."

"If Hood is right," Ronnie said, "we could be working together again. Nothing like a common enemy to make new friends."

Two hours later the second bottle was empty. Korov was singing a Spetsnaz marching song and trying to teach Nick and Lamont the words. Ronnie just shook his head. They were attracting attention. A large man walked over to them. He'd been drinking. It was the kind of bar where people drank a lot.

"Who's your Russki friend? He doesn't belong here."

"You don't like my singing? It's a good song."

"I don't like Russkis."

Nick emptied his glass. "This Russki earned the right to be here. So why don't you go finish your drink. I'm trying to learn a song."

Two more men walked over behind the first.

"Trouble, Joe?"

"Just someone who needs to leave. You're leaving, aren't you, pal? With your Russki asshole buddy here."

Nick sighed. He stood. Korov swayed a little and stood with him. Lamont stood, his arm still in a sling. Ronnie stood up on his crutches. He held one loose in his right hand.

"You're drunk. Why don't you drop it before you get hurt."

"Oh, how scary," the big man said. "Two cripples, a Russki and an asshole."

He swung. Nick blocked it easily with his left arm and hit him with a hard right twice in the face. He felt cartilage break. The man went backward over a table. His friends came in fast. Korov decked one. Ronnie took out the other with his crutch. Lamont watched. The bar erupted into a brawl.

It took a while to sort out. When it was done, the four of them were on the street. They were told they were no longer welcome at The Point. They were a little worse for wear. Ronnie's shiny new crutch was bent. It made him hobble as he walked.

"I was getting tired of that joint anyway." Lamont's eye was swelling.

"Just like Moscow," Korov said. They walked down the street laughing.

CHAPTER SIXTY-SEVEN

"What do you think?"

"Wow. This is great."

Selena stood with Nick in the living room of her new condo. Her condo, not theirs. Not yet. She'd had some things shipped from San Francisco. The rest was new. New paintings on the walls, new furniture.

She'd chosen antique rugs with geometric patterns of red and blue and cream. Stylized animals and trees and birds. The kitchen gleamed. A rack of shining pans hung ready over the center island and stove. She'd gone light brown leather for the chairs and couches. A few antiques, flowers. It was comfortable, inviting, a place you could live in and put your feet up. Selena was neat. She wasn't trying for House Beautiful.

"Wait till you see the bedroom."

"Why don't you show me?"

The bedroom was beautiful. A king-size bed with an elaborate headboard, soft pillows, smooth sheets. The Klee hung on the wall over the bed. They undressed. He held her against him. She reached down and took him in her hand. He felt life beating in her chest. Her body was warm. He molded against her, kissed her.

She pushed him down on the bed. She smiled and bent down to kiss him. He ran his hand down the taut curve of her back, over her buttocks. She lowered herself onto him. They made love slowly, taking their time. Afterwards they lay holding each other. She felt his heart pounding, unspoken tension in his body.

"Nice bedroom," he said.

"It's better with you in it."

"Selena..."

She got up and put on a green silk robe.

"I think I know what you're going to say."

She walked out of the room, came back with a bottle of wine and two glasses. She got back in bed. They sat with their backs against the headboard.

"So what am I going to say?"

"You're not ready to live together, are you?"

Nick took a glass from her. "No, I guess not. I've thought about it. A lot. At least when people weren't shooting at us."

"Bad joke."

"Yeah." He drank some wine. "I don't think it's a good idea, that's all."

"Neither do I."

"You don't?" She'd surprised him.

"You still aren't over Megan."

"Megan's gone."

"Not in your head, she isn't."

"I don't compare the two of you, if that's what you mean. I don't do that."

"I know. But she's still in there. I can feel it."

"It's just different with you. I love you, but it's different."

"It should be. It has to be. But you have to choose."

As she said the words she wished she hadn't.

"Choose? Between you and Megan? Selena, Megan's dead."

"Yes. She is. So maybe you need to get over it."

"You don't know a damn thing about Megan."

"I know enough to know she's a ghost between us. I know it would be a mistake to pretend she's not there. I know I love you but I need more back. Until you can do that, I don't see what point there'd be in moving in together."

Selena felt herself getting angry. *Damn it, this isn't how I wanted it to go.*

Nick set the wine on the end table and got up. He began putting on his clothes. He put on his shirt, strapped the shoulder rig on. Put on his jacket.

"I'm sorry. I'm working on it."

"Let me know when you've figured it out." Her tone was bitter. She heard the door close behind him.

Damn it! Damn it to hell!

She refused to cry.

CHAPTER SIXTY-EIGHT

President Rice looked at Harker and steepled his hands together. He had deep shadows under his eyes.

"The Pentagon?"

"Yes, sir. We went back in. Someone has removed all traces of Black Harvest from their computers. The scenario no longer exists. There's no trail, nothing to suggest it was ever contemplated."

"It could be CYA time on their part. Just in case someone made a connection in the press."

"I don't think so, Mr. President. Black Harvest was buried deep. No one outside the Pentagon could have found it. I suspect very few people over there even knew it existed."

"That is a very disturbing thought, Director."

"Yes, sir."

"It's very convenient, Lodge's suicide." Rice watched her.

"Yes, sir."

"That's all?"

She hadn't told him Hood had killed Lodge. Plausible deniability was sometimes more than a convenient phrase, regardless of the opinion of the media. Rice had created the Project to keep him informed, but in this case it really was something he didn't need to know.

"As you said, sir, it's very convenient."

Rice didn't pursue it. She didn't think he ever would.

"What do you think about Hood as the new DCI?"

That surprised her. "I think he would be an excellent choice, sir. He's up to speed on everything. He's well respected at the Agency. He's one of theirs. The transition would be smooth under him."

Elizabeth had briefed Rice on Hood's suspicions of a wider conspiracy crossing international borders. It hadn't made the President's day. She thought it was probably a factor in Rice's consideration of Hood as the next DCI.

"Director, it seems that every time you solve a problem something else turns up."

"Yes, sir, it does seem like that. I have a very good team. When you turn over rocks, things crawl out."

"I want you to pursue this. This possible conspiracy. You said Dansinger promised Lodge the White House."

She said nothing.

"Even in the current funding climate, that is not an easy thing to do. It takes more than money and influence. You still have to convince the American public."

"Apparently someone believes that's possible, Mr. President. Dansinger and Lodge were ready to kill millions of people to get what they wanted. Whoever is behind this didn't care much about that. I don't think anyone they tried to put in this office would care much either."

Rice rose. Elizabeth stood and waited.

"Find out who they are, Director."

"Yes, sir."

As she left the Oval Office she glanced back. Rice stood at the windows looking out over the White House lawn. Suddenly he seemed much older.

CHAPTER SIXTY-NIINE

This time when Nick saw the armored Cadillac waiting he simply got in when the driver held the door for him. The same back seat. The same luxury. The same black glass partition down the middle. The car moved silently into Washington traffic. The overhead halo lights cast a soft glow on the black leather interior.

"You've been busy." Adam's electronic voice came through the speaker grill.

"You could say that. How much do you know?"

"All of it. Well done."

"Who are you?"

"Think of me as an interested party."

"Interested in what?"

"In making sure AEON doesn't succeed."

"AEON?"

"The group behind Dansinger."

"So there is an organization."

"There definitely is an organization."

"Who are they?"

"A group of powerful men. AEON has been in existence for a long time. Their goal is control."

"Control?"

"Of everything. World domination."

"You're not going to start talking about the Illuminati or secret Masons are you?"

Laughter from the speaker. It sounded bizarre with the electronic distortion. "No, of course not. Those are convenient distractions to divert attention from the truth. But AEON is real. They mean business. You remember that little band of Nazis you broke up?"

"That was AEON?"

"One tentacle of it. They are not pleased with you and Harker and the others."

Nick leaned back in the leather. He waited. The car rolled through the streets, quiet, soft.

"Did they kill Dansinger?"

"Yes. He screwed up. Your raid in Texas told them he was exposed. They couldn't let him live. His public execution sends a message to everyone in their organization."

"What are they planning to do?"

"About Dansinger? Nothing. It's done."

"I meant now that their plan has been stopped."

"Their plan never stops. They simply move past failures to something else. When we know more I'll contact you."

"Who are they?"

"Their leader is Malcolm Foxworth."

"The media guy? With the newspapers?

"Yes. They are international. Dansinger was the newest addition to their ruling council. One of two Americans. They will replace him."

"Who's the other American?"

"We don't know. He may be highly placed in the Pentagon. We know they are embedded there, but we don't know if one of the council is directly involved."

"Jesus."

"Anatoly Orgorov is another member of the leadership council. The Russian Foreign Minister."

Nick thought about that. Harker was not going to be thrilled when he told her about this conversation.

"Henri Maupassant is the Minister of Finance in France. He has been part of the council for the last ten years."

"Maupassant? He's a key player in the European debt crisis."

"Exactly. You begin to see, I think."

Nick did. "Who are the others?"

"We're not sure of their identities. There is someone in Brazil, China, Japan. Germany. Possibly India. That is the leadership. The structure is a pyramid, with Foxworth at the top, the council below him. Below them is another layer of perhaps a hundred. Below them, thousands. We don't know how many."

The Cadillac moved like a silent omen through the unseen streets of Washington.

"What have they done in the past?"

"AEON worked carefully with Hitler to groom him for his role. He was a pawn, though he didn't know it. The assassination of Kennedy was engineered by them and we got Vietnam. They were quite active in the 60s. Napoleon received their backing. They arranged the death of the Archduke Ferdinand in 1914. They sank the Lusitania. Need I go on?""

"That's hard to believe."

"Of course it is. They count on that. Circumstances can be arranged, things made to appear different than they are. Look at how Rice covered up the events about Senator Greenwood."

"Are you saying Rice is part of this?"

"No. He is not. I merely bring it up as an example. Leaders and governments often conceal unpleasant truths from the public. Sometimes there's a legitimate reason. When there isn't, they make one up. In the case of something as public and high profile as the Kennedy affair, people who might actually upset things are eliminated. Others are labeled as misguided or as conspiracy nuts. There are plenty of those. It works quite well to deflect attention from the truth. Especially in our digital age."

The car slowed and rolled to a stop.

"Why have you told me this? What do you expect me to do?"

"What you and the Project do so well. You are uniquely positioned to stop AEON. We will help in every way we can. I advise you to be careful. They are certain to respond."

"We can't just go after someone like Foxworth or the Russian Foreign Minister. Jesus, Adam."

"You'll find a way."

The door opened.

"Who are you?" Nick asked again. There was no answer.

Nick got out and watched the car drive away. The street was deserted. He was suddenly cold, aware that he was alone. He didn't like the feeling. It felt as though the night was full of eyes. Sometimes it seemed like everyone was watching him. CIA. The Russians. Adam, whoever the hell he was. Maybe AEON. AEON raised the stakes beyond anything he'd run into before. If Adam was telling the truth.

He didn't like feeling alone.

He thought about what Selena had said about Megan. A ghost between them. It was almost nine years since she'd died. Nine years of living with a ghost.

He took out his wallet, took out the picture of Megan he kept there. The picture was creased and faded. It was just a picture, its only value the memories it stirred. Looking at it, he realized he felt nothing. No, that wasn't right. It was something, but it was distant, a memory of a memory. It wasn't Megan.

Everyone ends up in the same place.

He was still here. Selena was here. Megan was gone. He'd thought he'd gotten past it. He'd thought he'd let her go, but he hadn't. Selena was right about Megan. She was right about a lot of things.

He could have a ghost or he could have her. What kind of choice was that?

He'd told her he was afraid she'd be killed. Thinking about it, he felt that he was on the edge of something, some recognition he didn't want to see, some feeling he didn't want to have. It was true, what he'd said to her, but it wasn't that simple.

She loves me.

His mind opened a door.

It's her pain I'm afraid of, not mine.

I'm the one I think will get killed.

I don't want to hurt her.

I really do love her.

The realization was a physical blow to his chest. He'd been pushing away the deeper fear of his own death. Of causing her the kind of pain he'd felt when he lost Megan. It sent a shiver over his body, rippled down his spine. Selena had got past the barriers. It was too late to throw up the wall again.

He couldn't stop doing what he did to try and keep them both safe. Not after what Adam had told him. Now there was another, darker enemy.

AEON.

Now that I know, I can tell her. She'll understand.

He took out his phone and called her.

The Nostradamus File

Book Six in the PROJECT Series is coming mid-summer 2013...

Blog: http://www.alexlukeman.blogspot.com

Website: http://www.alexlukeman.org